Penalty

Paul Cockburn

The right of Paul Cockburn to be identified as the author
of this work has been asserted by him in accordance with
the Copyright, Designs and Patents Act 1988.

Virgin

With thanks to Rod & Wendy

First published in Great Britain in 1997 by
Virgin Books
an imprint of Virgin Publishing Ltd
332 Ladbroke Grove
London W10 5AH

A catalogue record for this book is available from the
British Library.

ISBN 0 7535 0093 0

Typeset by Galleon Typesetting, Ipswich
Printed and bound by
BPC Paperbacks Ltd, Aylesbury

One

Jazz was down. Nicky was off in the distance somewhere, trapped. Chris hadn't seen Mac for quite a while.

He bit his lip and took a deep breath, trying to stay calm. In the darkness ahead, he could make out a shape moving stealthily through the doorway. Smoke drifted across the room like mist, swirling as the stranger crouched low, looking across to his left. Chris's eyes were becoming used to the deep gloom, and he could see that the intruder was a tall, heavily built man. He moved with a curious, crab-like gait across the soft floor. Chris felt sure he knew him.

Chris remained still, patient. The man hadn't really searched the room and Chris wasn't certain his hiding place would conceal him from a more probing examination. As he had feared, the man paused close to the second door, glancing behind him before he went through.

Chris froze. In his hands, the unfamiliar weight of the gun was solid and harsh. He knew what he had to do.

Having finished a quick sweep of the room, the man prepared to step over the threshold of the second door. At that very second, Chris leapt up from his hiding place, aimed the weapon and pulled the trigger. The man's broad back was a clear, open target. Chris gave him a long burst, then dived through the first door, without waiting to see the result of his ambush. The only thing that mattered now was to escape . . .

The control panel lights on the top of the laser went out, leaving just the small LCD with his score showing. Chris read it as he made his way towards the exit – plus 260. That last hit on Uncle Fabian had scored over 100 points.

Most of the others were already outside by the time Chris

came through the flap. The attendant unfastened the velcro straps on his 'armour' and relieved him of the weapon.

'Two hundred and sixty,' said the guy. 'Looks like you kids won!'

'Yes!!!' cheered Nicky. Being on the winning side counted for a lot more than the fact that his own score was minus 500. Nicky had been eliminated along with one of his cousins, Jazz and Mac's father.

At that moment, Nicky's Uncle Fabian came out through the flap across the entrance of the large inflatable maze. He was the last of them to appear. The Photon Tag operator removed his gear with practised ease. 'Minus 500,' he announced. 'You're supposed to come out when you're eliminated, you know.'

'It happened right at the end,' Uncle Fabian said, with a serious expression on his face. 'That little bushwhacker jumped me just before time ran out.' His finger stretched out in Chris's direction.

That only made Nicky laugh louder. 'Don't be such a sore loser, Uncle! I'm not complaining about the way you and Paulo held me down while Luke shot me in the back!' Nicky's uncle and two cousins had gone round in a pack for the first five minutes, trying to use their physical strength to capture the boys and blast them at point blank range.

The Photon Tag operator looked up from kitting out one of the next batch of kids, giving Uncle Fabian a look that said he considered picking on kids poor sport. He had told Chris while they were waiting that he was a kick-boxing champion who ran the Photon Tag game as a day job. Not the sort of guy anyone would want to cross – even though he wasn't much more than one and a half metres tall. The guy was all muscle and looked as hard as nails.

'Three of you eliminated and two of us!' crowed Nicky. 'The boys win!'

Jazz and Robbie joined in the cheering. It was easy for them, they weren't related to anyone on the losing side. Chris knew Nicky's family well enough to realise that his cousins would take the loss badly all afternoon.

Chris's father was already leading the group away from the inflatable bubble. Nicky was all for another run through, but the queue outside had grown even longer than before. It was time to check out what else was on offer besides shooting their parents and other relatives with a laser.

Almost at once, Chris spotted a large sign, hung from poles between two caravans. At once he knew exactly what they should do next. In fact, he had been expecting to see something like it from the moment they had arrived at the fair. He grinned with satisfaction and pointed it out to the others.

Every city has some event that marks it out as unusual, some special day in the calendar that it celebrates alone. Cambridge has the May Balls; Nottingham has Goose Fair; everywhere has something.

The city of Oldcester has one of the strangest. In the middle of the autumn – when the weather is often cold and wet, it has the 'Equinox Mystery Fair'.

Not only is it a tradition that the weather is awful, but there is actually a local by-law which says no-one is allowed to advertise where the fair is taking place. It was all something to do with a petition to King Henry VI. The local market was held outside the town and the shopkeepers complained that they were losing trade. Henry, not a king noted for his sense of humour, decreed that the wool merchants and other traders could have their fair, but they weren't allowed to tell anyone where it was being held.

Local historians reckoned Henry VI must have been angry with the leaders of the city – which was no more than a small town in those days – since they supported the other side in the Wars of the Roses. Chris, along with his mates at Spirebrook Comprehensive on the outskirts of the city, preferred to think that the daft old King had just got fed up with people moaning and bleating, and had decided to have a laugh.

So, each year, on the weekend closest to the equinox, when night and day are of equal length, Oldcester has a massive fair – and makes a big point of not talking about it. No-one puts up any signs or posters; the local radio and TV stations try to pretend the location of the fair is a big secret; actors dress up in medieval costume and wander the streets threatening to fine anyone they catch talking about it. One year, someone had had the idea of putting up AA road direction signs which read EQUINOX MYSTERY FAIR in black lettering at the top, followed by a large question mark.

In Oldcester's neighbouring towns and cities, they thought the whole thing was barmy. What was the point of having a huge great fair if nobody knew where it was going to be held?

Which was missing the point. Everyone in Oldcester always knew where the fair was going to be held. For one thing, there were only a few locations around the city where it could be staged. For another, it was hard to keep a secret involving the arrival of huge fairground rides, a massive sound stage and 3,000 seats, plus hundreds of smaller stalls. Also, the police tended to cheat by directing traffic off the motorway towards the fair, which showed *they* knew.

True, there had been confusion in the past. There were stories about an equinox fair in the 1700s which had been shrouded in a mist so dense people had assumed they were in the wrong place and had given up looking. Plus the infamous year of 1866, when there had been rival fairs on two separate sites. (A riot had broken out at one, but a cavalry regiment, stationed near the city, had been sent to the other by mistake.)

But these days there was never any doubt. The marquees and stalls were erected on Thursday and long before Saturday dawned the whole city knew exactly where the 'Mystery Fair' was going to be.

In fact, the only confusion caused by the Equinox Mystery Fair came when people pretended they knew what was going on months in advance, even when it was obvious that they didn't have a clue. It was a bluffing game everyone in the city took part in. It was just a bit of fun.

After all, some people love a mystery more than anything else.

4

TWO

On the Saturday before the fair, Chris Stephens woke early, and was about to jump out of bed when it struck him – he didn't have to rush anywhere.

He savoured that thought for a moment. He could hear his father downstairs, making breakfast and getting ready to go to work. Normally, Chris would get up early, and by the time his father went off to work, Chris would be getting stuck into some homework or other chores. Not that Chris was keen on hoovering or studying, but time was always short, even at the weekends.

In fact, especially at the weekends.

Today, though, he didn't have to be anywhere until midday. He could easily just lie in bed for a few hours and catch up with some well-earned res–

The telephone warbled. The sound cut through the quiet of the house like a knife, cutting away at the silence every couple of seconds. Chris groaned. The phone had destroyed any chance of him getting back to sleep. Chris knew it would be for him.

'Chris!' his father bellowed upstairs.

'It's Nicky . . .' Chris muttered.

'It's Nicky!'

If it had been anyone else, Chris might have got away with 'tell them I'll call back', but Nicky wouldn't be fobbed off. Whatever Nicky was calling about, it wouldn't wait. Nicky's whole life was lived at the last moment.

With one last yawn, more from habit than because he was still sleepy, Chris dragged himself out of bed. His reflection in the mirror on the inside of his open wardrobe door looked more dead than alive, and Chris knew how it felt. He stared at himself for a moment. He was tall, quite slender (although he had put on a little weight in the last year – all muscle, he told himself) but ordinary-looking. He had a shaggy mop of fair hair, which exploded in every direction; his eyes were blue, and they didn't always appear half-closed and blurry. Some of the other guys at school were experimenting with moustaches – one hair at a time, in Chris's opinion – but his skin was smooth, pale and untouched by any marks save a chicken pox scar in the middle of his forehead.

Having convinced himself that he was who he thought he was, Chris pulled on his jeans and staggered downstairs to be met by his father standing in the hall and holding the receiver as if he had been frightened to put it down.

'Tea?' asked Chris's father.

'Can't you make it?' Chris replied, his brain still functioning at less than 50 per cent efficiency.

Mr Stephens rolled his eyes, then handed the phone over and went out into the kitchen. Chris put the receiver to his ear and managed to grunt 'Yes?' into the mouthpiece.

'Were you still asleep?' asked Nicky, managing to make it sound as if Chris had been in bed for the last three days.

'Don't tell anyone, OK? I'd hate anyone to know I go to bed in the middle of the night.'

'It's 8.00 am!' Nicky informed him. Even the sound of the time made Chris feel exhausted. Nicky, on the other hand, sounded wide awake.

But then, when didn't he? Nicky was Chris's closest friend. They'd been through a lot together. On a rising scale of excitement: they went to the same school (Spirebrook Comprehensive); they supported the same football team (Oldcester United, currently proving that teams promoted from Division One of the Whoever-Is-Sponsoring-It-This-Year League don't always go straight back down from the Premiership); they were both in United's youth team; and they had been involved in some pretty wild adventures. These were typical kids' stuff like getting kidnapped by a local villain, chased by an American gangster and arrested for (1) hitting a guy over the head with a drum and (2) burning down part of the school. Chris liked to believe Nicky was to blame for all the bad bits of these shared experiences. This was a bit rich considering that he and Nicky hadn't even been in the same country during one recent escapade, but Chris didn't let that stop him.

'I don't remember booking an alarm call, Nicky.'

6

Nicky laughed. 'Have you forgotten? We're going out!'

'We are?'

'You remember!' Nicky insisted. With each sentence, his voice was getting higher and louder, as if he was worried that Chris had lost his mind or been brainwashed. 'We talked about it at school yesterday.'

Friday was a complete blank as far as Chris was concerned. Football training had been tougher than usual, he knew that. Even if he had forgotten, his stiff, sore muscles would have reminded him eventually.

All the same, he managed to recall Nicky talking about plans for Saturday morning. Chris knew he must have missed the bit where he agreed to go along with them.

'Are you talking about this stupid idea to check out Horton's Meadow?'

'Of course!' cried Nicky, relieved that he was talking to Chris, and not to some zombie inhabiting Chris's body.

Right then, Chris would have settled for being one of the undead. Joining Nicky on one of his mad jaunts was bad enough when he was wide awake. Just now, the thought of dragging himself out to Horton's Meadow – a charming name for a boggy, thorn-covered stretch of land on the far side of the river – was about as appealing as playing catch with a scorpion. Chris slowly remembered just what Nicky's idea was.

The Oldcester Equinox Mystery Fair was just a week away. There were two traditions connected with the fair every kid in Oldcester knew about. On the Monday morning after the fair, those lucky enough to live nearby went there as early as they could, just as the trailers and lorries and cars were setting off. From first light, small groups of kids would be seen all over the site, searching the trodden grass for money. Everyone knew loads of money was spilled during the weekend; everyone knew someone who had found twenty or thirty quid. Nicky Fiorentini claimed he'd found a ten pound note one year.

The second tradition was, that in the week before the fair, everyone tried to find out where it would be held and how they could get in for free. Elaborate diagrams were made of holes in fences, ditches, hidden footpaths and other possible entrances. Anything rather than pay at the gate.

This being the Saturday before the fair, Nicky could only be talking about one thing.

'Horton's Meadow, Nicky? They aren't going to hold the fair there, are they? The last time they used it, it rained all weekend and the place flooded. There were trailers stuck in the mud a week later.'

Chris could picture Nicky's face on the other end of the line. It would be wearing his injured expression, the one he put on when people started picking holes in one of his grand ideas. Only really boring people used logic in a situation like this as far as Nicky was concerned.

'Ah, but that's where you're wrong!' Nicky countered. 'Everyone tells that story, but it wasn't that bad. And the council did a lot of work a few years back to –'

Chris cut him off. He'd abandoned the mental picture of Nicky looking wounded. For one thing, it sounded as if Nicky's mouth was half-full. That meant he was eating breakfast while he was talking (which made Chris's stomach rumble). For another, an explanation like that didn't sound like it came directly out of Nicky's brain.

'How do you know all this, Nicky?'

Nicky sounded sickeningly smug. 'Mac's father,' he whispered (as if he was passing on an important secret). 'You know, he works for the council.'

Chris knew that very well. Mac was another one of the Spirebrook football mafia. He was one year younger than Chris and about five years shorter, but he had turned out to be a more than decent defensive midfielder. A kind of Paul Ince without the whingeing.

As for Mac's father, he was the boss of the Architects and Surveyors Department of Oldcester City Council. In Nicky's eyes, this meant he was the perfect source for information about the location for this year's Mystery Fair.

'And what has Mr MacIntyre told you?'

Chris heard Nicky hesitate. 'Uh – well, he hasn't actually said anything,' Fiorentini said slowly.

Chris could feel himself growing older waiting for Nicky to get to the point. At that moment, his father came out of the kitchen, holding a mug of tea in one hand and the previous afternoon's local newspaper in the other. Chris saw the headline on the back page: UNITED'S MYSTERY PORTUGUESE SIGNING – WILL HE COSTA LOT?

Ho, ho.

8

Chris reached out and took the mug. His father looked up, looked at his empty hand, then looked up at the ceiling. He turned round and went back to the kitchen.

'OK, Nicky,' sighed Chris after he had taken a sip of the scalding hot tea. 'Explain. But just the highlights, OK? No action replays or Alan Hansen comments, OK?'

'OK. You know Russell Jones comes past Horton's Meadow on his way to school?' Chris nodded, taking another sip. Then he realised that Nicky wouldn't have seen the gesture and gasped 'Yes!' while trying to blow steam off his tongue.

'Well, on his way to school, he saw Mac's dad on the meadow. Twice. Taking measurements and stuff.'

'So?'

'So, it's obvious, isn't it? It must be because they're using the meadow for the fair! And Russell says there are a couple of hidden gaps in the hedges around it where we could sneak in.'

That sounded OK. Chris had no objection in principle to sneaking into the fair. True, it usually only cost 25p to get in anyway, but it was traditional that you avoided paying if you could. And it had been a long time since the fair had been held anywhere near Spirebrook.

'Fine. So, Russell can show us the way in, right?'

Nicky replied very quickly, as if he was getting impatient. 'Don't be boring, Chris! We have to take a look for ourselves. Come on, this'll be fun.'

Chris could feel his strength ebbing. It was going to be easier to agree with Nicky in the long run. At the same time, this was his one morning off . . .

He made one last plea, knowing it was hopeless. 'OK, OK. But do we have to do this today, Nicky?'

He knew the answer before Fiorentini said a word. When else would they have time? It was this morning or never.

Thirty minutes later, Chris was putting on his coat, searching for his keys and opening the front door. As always, he'd ended up doing what Nicky wanted in the first place. If there was such a thing as reincarnation, Chris knew he had done something really bad in his previous life to come back in this one with Nicky Fiorentini as his best mate.

The gang met up outside Tescos, on the corner of the junction where the main road crosses Church Hill and the new road that runs behind Spirebrook Comprehensive. Nicky and Mac came down Church Hill from their respective homes up the steep rise; Robert James stepped off the bus at the corner; and Chris and Jazz, having met up outside the restaurant/shop run by Jazz's family, strolled along the main road. They were due to meet Russell on the other side of the river, near the meadow.

Anyone watching this particular crew gathering might have wondered what linked them together. On the face of it, they were quite an odd bunch. Out of school uniform, and with no-one else to worry about how he looked, Chris was his usual scruffy self – hair springing out in every direction and baseball jacket worn over a football shirt and faded old jeans. Nicky, teeth gleaming as he smiled at the others, was more smartly turned out, thanks to his older sister's new job at a clothes shop. Although his hair was neatly combed back, the long fringe fell across his eyes every few moments and had to be pushed back with (he thought) an elegant sweep of his hand. Jazz was all in black, wearing a Red Dwarf T-shirt under a leather jacket. As always, he looked uneasy among his friends, dreading the prospect of getting into trouble. His father didn't let him out much on Saturdays, preferring him to work in the shop. Jazz was wondering if this was the best way to spend his few hours of freedom.

These three were classmates, though there was no obvious way of telling that. Nicky was shorter than the other two – certainly Chris stood a good head above him – and not much taller than Robert James, who was two years younger. James's face was completely clear and unblemished and there was less confidence in his eyes, which made him look younger. At the same time, he was powerfully built, with strong legs and wide shoulders. He moved like a leopard, light on his feet.

The last of the quintet, Donald 'Mac' MacIntyre, was the smallest of the bunch, though he fell between James and the other three in age. He was wearing a thick jumper and jeans, as if winter had sneaked up on him earlier than anyone else.

Different in size, looks, colouring and clothing, they made a curious sight gathered together. The Asian Brit, the Scot, the semi-Italian, the recent arrival and the born and bred local boy. There was no obvious link between them.

But in fact there were two, or perhaps three.

'Is this going to take long?' asked Jazz.

Nicky gave him a hard stare. 'What's your problem?'

'I've got homework to finish,' Jazz began. 'My father's giving me a hard time about the mocks . . .'

He stopped, aware that Chris and Nicky were facing the same set of exams, although in different circumstances. 'I mean, it's not long now, is it?' he finished, lamely.

'Give me a break,' muttered Nicky.

'Well, have you done that geography assignment?' Jazz asked. Chris almost stifled a mocking laugh, at which point Nicky glared at him. Everyone knew that geography figured in Nicky's plans in much the same way as Vinnie Jones figured in Glenn Hoddle's as first choice for midfield playmaker.

'Have you done it?' Nicky snapped quickly.

'Almost,' Chris replied. 'But I'm like Jazz, I can't spend a lot of time mucking about today.'

'I know, I know!' Nicky responded hotly. He gestured along the road, as if to say that the sooner they started the sooner they could get back to ignoring geography homework.

At the back of the group, Mac innocently asked what homework Robert James had over the weekend.

'Some English,' James answered. 'I did it last night.'

Nicky's head snapped round and he gave the two younger boys his patented 'keep-this-up-and-you-die' dirty look. As they continued along the main road, Mac nudged James and whispered something about exams making the others cranky.

So, that was one thing that linked them together – school. All five were students at Spirebrook Comprehensive, which lay behind the supermarket, tucked inside the sweeping curve of the river. The school consisted of three plain glass and concrete teaching blocks, a gym and some smaller buildings plus a peanut-shaped playing field crossed by electricity pylons and cables.

The school wasn't visible from the main road, not that any of the five looked for it. Spirebrook inspired a strange loyalty – nothing to do with buildings, teachers or lessons. 'Brookers knew they would never be at the top of the heap – the important thing was to avoid ending up at the bottom.

'We aren't going to be able to stay long, not if we're going to eat before practice,' Chris said to Nicky as they walked briskly towards the solid stone bridge, which carried the road over the sluggish, dark waters of the river.

Nicky shrugged as if he hadn't given it much thought. 'We could get something to eat in the city,' he decided. 'Do you have enough money?'

Chris searched his pockets and showed what he had – about eight pounds. Barely enough to keep Nicky in snacks.

'Tell you what, we'll go back to my place first and get Uncle Fabian to drive us to the ground. That'll be easiest, and with four of us we'll save a fortune on bus fares.'

There wasn't the slightest doubt in Nicky's mind that his family would rally round. Three extra hungry mouths for lunch and a spot of chauffeuring? All in a day's work for the Fiorentinis.

There was an empty Pepsi can on the pavement just ahead. Nicky sprinted forward and pounced on it as if he was robbing an opposing full back instead of a lamppost. He flicked the 'ball' back to Chris who trapped it on his instep and flicked it aside to Jazz. With a lazy, elegant swing of his left foot, Jazz chipped the can back at Nicky who took it on his thigh, spinning round to face the front again.

An old woman with a shopping trolley blocked his path. Nicky saw her at the last second, and mistimed his next touch, sending the can clattering between the decorative rails of the bridge and spinning down towards the distant water.

There was a long moment when the woman looked at Nicky and then past him over the rail, as if she was about to lecture him for being a noisy hooligan and a litterbug.

'You want to keep your eyes open,' she said in a sour voice, then she added crisply: 'I didn't even tackle you.'

The others were already laughing. When the woman added: 'Throw-in to the grandmas,' they were helpless with hysterical glee.

'It's not that funny,' Nicky muttered as soon as the old woman was out of earshot. He was on his own there.

Three

They met up with Russell at the end of the road that led to his home. Not that it was much of a road — more an unpaved track that quickly vanished between high hedgerows and tall beech trees. The cars on the main road passed it by without a single driver so much as noticing that it was there.

Russell was sitting on the arm of an old bench. The wooden seat had rotted away, and weeds grew through the iron framework. Russell was throwing pebbles at the dandelions, making the seeds explode with each direct hit.

He looked up as he saw the others coming towards him. He recognised at once that Nicky had the hump about something, but he ignored it. Instead he focused on Chris and the others.

'I was beginning to think you guys weren't coming,' he said as soon as they were close enough to hear.

'We had a game of football on the way,' replied Chris. He was struggling to stop himself laughing. Mac and Jazz weren't even fighting it; both had tears in their eyes.

It's never easy coming in late when others are already caught up in a fit of the giggles. Russell decided he wouldn't bother trying. Nicky's pout made it quite obvious who the butt of the joke was.

'Come on,' Nicky snapped as he swept past the bench, 'we don't have all day.' He was twenty metres up the lane before any of the others had started to follow him.

Walking alongside Chris, Russell could hear Jazz and Mac chuckling and whispering. Robert James had joined in too, now that he was out of Nicky's direct sight. Russell tried to listen in, but the conversation didn't make sense — they seemed to be picking the strikers for a grannies' eleven.

Chris was still grinning as well, but at least he looked

capable of speaking. Russell gave it a few seconds, and then tried to start a conversation.

'Did you see the paper?'

'Yeah,' said Chris. He knew what Russell was talking about. 'What do you think?'

Chris shrugged. 'Maybe there's something in it, I don't know. You remember what Dennis Lively said during Euro 96? If he could buy a whole team, he'd buy the Germans; if he could only get one guy, he'd pick a Portuguese player.'

Russell nodded, remembering the remark. However, since then, Oldcester United's larger-than-life chairman had written out a cheque for £1.9 million to sign Luis Rodriguez from Barcelona, which mopped up a good chunk of the cash Oldcester received from their new sponsorship deal with Virgin Cola. The brooding Spaniard might not have given the same electric shock to Oldcester's fortunes that Cantona had given Manchester United, but he was still the biggest overseas name attracted to Star Park – ever.

'My guess is the paper has it wrong,' Chris told Russell, 'unless we're going to be the first team in the Premiership with sponsors on our shorts . . .'

They walked along the next stretch of the lane in silence. United were playing away that afternoon, at Leeds, which was a fixture that always seemed to bring out the best in both Uniteds. Chris would have loved to have gone, but he had other commitments.

By the time Russell spoke again, they were almost at the point where the lane crossed a paved road.

'Has Nicky told you what I saw?' Russell asked.

Once again, Chris knew what Russell was talking about, although it took him a second longer this time. 'What? Oh, right, yeah. Mac's dad taking measurements.'

'What do you think?'

Chris gave his head a small shake as if he was shaking it clear of some other thought, then fixed his eyes on Jones. 'I don't know. It's probably nothing to do with the fair.' His eyes narrowed as they passed into the shadow of a particularly broad tree. 'I'd forgotten how narrow this lane is . . .'

It had been a while since he and Nicky had been out this way. When Russell had first appeared, they hadn't trusted him at all. So, they had tried to find out more about him by spying

14

on him. This was the route they had followed on their way back from a successful piece of scouting, which had uncovered some stolen goods belonging to Sean Priest, the bearded youth team manager at Oldcester United.

Of course, the boys had been lost at the time, so Chris hadn't paid much attention to the lane itself. Since then, he had been back this way only once or twice, on his way to Russell's place. All he really knew about the lane was that it joined a slightly wider, paved road after about a mile. Russell's house was off to the right across the fields, a lonely, broken-down old dump in the middle of nowhere. There was a posh private school somewhere to the left, between the lane they were following and the main road. The paved road linked the school to a village. On the other side, the track continued, and after a fork it reached Horton's Meadow.

Russell looked around, although he knew the lane better than anyone. It was the route he took to school every morning. Chris was suddenly struck by the thought that this included dark mornings and gloomy afternoons. His mind went back to the idea that had started to surface before.

'There's no way they'll get much traffic up here . . .' he said quietly, almost to himself.

'What?'

Chris turned his head to face Russell.

'What other ways are there on to Horton's Meadow?'

Russell considered this quickly. 'Well, there's School Lane.'

'That's the road that runs between that posh kids' school and West Graves, right?' Russell nodded. 'But that doesn't actually connect to the main road, does it?' Chris continued.

'Well, sure, eventually,' Russell informed him, making a small sketch on the palm of one hand. 'After it goes through West Graves, it twists round and then goes up to the B6555 . . .'

Chris got the point. 'What I meant was that there's no connection between the school end of the lane and the main road. So anyone driving from Oldcester to the meadow is going to have to go all round the houses to get there.'

Russell was about to point out that there weren't that many houses, but he knew what Chris was driving at.

'There's no way the city would pick Horton's Meadow for the fair,' Chris insisted, 'not if people can't get there by car.' He looked forward. Nicky was still pulling away, kicking stones along the lane and ignoring the rest of them as if they didn't exist.

'They used to use it though,' Russell said, which caused Chris to pause just before he called out to Nicky.

'That was back in the fifties or something,' Chris said. 'There used to be a railway line over the river and a station at West Graves. I've seen pictures.'

In fact, Chris remembered, the old metal swing bridge where the railway crossed the river was still there, a dark, thick and heavy structure a few hundred metres downstream from the slightly more elegant road bridge. It was fenced off and all the external ramps and ladders had been taken away. When the new road had been built, there had been plans to knock it down, but it would have cost a lot money to do that, and some people in the area actually liked the ugly old thing.

Not Chris, but that was another story.

'Yeah, you can still see where the lines ran,' Russell commented, gesturing off past the trees.

Russell knew the country over here really well. When they had first met, Russell had been in the habit of getting backwards and forwards across the river by means of a vast grey pipe that arched across it. The pipe was another left-over, this time from an abandoned and demolished chemical works. Several of their adventures had taken place near the river – and Chris had almost ended two of them (and his life) by falling in. The memories made him shiver.

'So, you think this is a wild-goose chase?' Russell was asking.

Chris shook himself loose of the thoughts that had been flying around his mind. He didn't like the prickling feeling at the back of his neck.

'It has to be. They can't route the traffic from the fair all the way round to the other side of the meadow – and it's not like the road is that great over there, is it? Mac's dad must be doing something else, like maybe –'

It hit him like a slap to the face. For no reason at all, the idea that had just popped into his mind made him feel quite angry.

'Hang on a minute!' he snapped, spinning round on the spot. Coming up behind, Mac, Jazz and Robbie came to a sudden halt. 'Why are we doing this? Why haven't you just asked your dad if Horton's Meadow is where the fair is going to be?'

Mac, who was the target of this particular question, opened

16

his eyes wide with surprise. The others looked a bit strung out too, but that was mostly because they were amazed no-one had thought of asking Mac's father sooner.

'He couldn't tell me, Chris. It's a secret.'

Chris dismissed that argument with a mocking laugh. 'Yeah, right – the worst-kept secret in Oldcester! Are you telling me your father would keep it a secret from you?'

Mac shrugged to show that he hadn't thought of asking.

'It's not like it's a really important decision,' Jazz pointed out. He realised at once Mac might take this as some kind of comment about the importance of his father's job and tried to put it right without success.

Chris took up the baton. 'Look, Mac, the idea that the location is a secret is just a stupid tradition. It's all anyone talks about for weeks! Don't tell me your dad hasn't said anything!'

'But he hasn't,' Mac protested, 'honest!'

'And you haven't asked?'

'Nicky said I shouldn't . . .' Mac began, and with those few words Chris's heart sank.

'Go on . . .' he sighed.

The five of them stopped in the middle of the lane. Mac looked quickly around the other faces.

'Nicky said if I just asked my dad, then he'd know we were planning to sneak in. Then he might not let me go.'

Mac clearly believed this was a possibility. Chris's dad might occasionally turn a blind eye to his son's escapades; the Fiorentini clan might even join in when Nicky was up to something, but Mac's father wasn't the kind of guy to put up with Mac getting into any kind of scrape. Except . . .

Except this was the Equinox Mystery Fair. Kids sneaked in any way they could – without paying. It was as much a part of the tradition as the nonsense about keeping the location secret. And Mac's dad hadn't exactly forced Mac to stay at home any of the previous years.

'This is nuts,' Chris muttered, and he was about ready to suggest they turn back when two things happened. First, he remembered Nicky was off up ahead. Second, they all heard the sound of an approaching motorbike.

Over the next few seconds, they forgot the idea of turning back completely. In some ways they'd all come to regret it.

Four

The motorcycle took a while to get up to them. The engine was so rough that its grumbling, coughing roar reached them through the quiet country air fifteen or twenty seconds before the bike appeared around the last corner.

The boys pressed themselves against the hedge. The bike was moving quite fast, but the rider had a clear view of them along a fairly straight piece of the lane. They felt the wind buffet them as he thundered past and a small cloud of dust and small stones flew up in his wake.

The bike was a grimy old Suzuki and it had a passenger on the pillion as well as the guy up front. Neither was wearing a helmet. The driver was wearing a heavy, black jacket, unzipped to show a ripped white T-shirt underneath. He had long blond hair whipping back past his ears; he wore wide aviator's goggles with blue lenses. Chris could see his teeth bared in a wide grin as he flashed past.

He didn't have such a good view of the passenger. All he could really be sure of was that he was a big guy in a long leather coat. He wore a blue bandanna around his mouth, a reversed baseball cap jammed tightly on his head and a pair of round-framed mirrored shades. He turned to face the boys, twisting his head back as the bike left them behind.

Chris stared back. For a moment, there was some small, nagging worry in the back of his mind. It was almost as if he had been able to see the man's eyes through the reflective glasses. And those eyes had been full of hatred.

Chris shook himself to drive the anxiety away. He wasn't going to get freaked out just because the guy was a biker.

The boys pulled themselves away from the hedge. Up ahead, the bike slid precariously as it came off the dirt and on to the paved road, making the turn almost a shade too fast. It vanished from view.

'I wonder who they were?' asked Jazz, who had a greater mistrust of men on bikes than Chris.

'Dunno,' Chris replied quietly.

'They'll prang that old heap taking corners like that,' Russell said. There was a slight edginess in his voice that Chris didn't like the sound of. Before he could think about it, however, Mac suddenly yelped: 'Nicky!' He looked around in alarm. 'What if he doesn't hear them coming?'

Chris was about to say that a deaf man in a soundproof box with double-glazing on his ears would hear that tortured old engine (even if he was in a Nicky-style sulk), when there was a screech of tyres from up ahead. The boys flinched, dreading the sound of an impact. It never came.

All the same, they ran to the corner, on to the road, and then quickly dog-legged left again to where the lane continued. As they rounded the second corner they heard an ugly, sharp, piercing voice screeching in rage.

'Are you mental? Doesn't this thing have a horn?'

Thank goodness, thought Chris. Nicky's all right.

They closed the gap to where Nicky was standing, parked across the road, fists on his hips. He was right in the face of the guy on the bike, who had removed his goggles and was listening to Nicky's outburst with some amazement. A long scar in the earth track showed where the bike had slewed sideways as it stopped.

Nicky looked up as his mates drew closer.

'This moron almost ran me over!' he yelled.

The guy looked back at Chris, his face still split in a wide, bright grin, like a model in a toothpaste commercial or an actor in an Aussie soap. He smoothed his hair back from his face, highlighting how tanned his skin was. He scratched at a few days' worth of beard and licked a dry patch on his lip.

'You didn't hear me coming?' he said, and Chris noticed the lazy, rolling accent.

Nicky wasn't prepared for this to be his fault. 'What difference would it have made?' he yelled. 'You came round that corner like Damon Hill.'

The guy was still grinning. He looked back past the other five – barely glancing at them – gesturing towards the corner.

'We weren't going that fast, mate,' he said, 'but we lost some grip coming back on to the dirt. It probably looked like we were out of control.'

Jazz touched Chris's elbow and nodded down towards the bike's rear tyre. There was next to no tread on it.

'I didn't expect to see anyone down here,' the guy said. 'It looked like a pretty quiet lane.'

'It was till you came down it,' Nicky said sourly, but it looked as if he didn't have the energy to stay mad much longer.

The man chuckled as if Nicky had made a really good joke. 'Well, no harm done. Listen, mind if I get back to my mates now? I'm dying of thirst.'

Nicky's eyes flashed. Chris knew he was still waiting for an apology. It wouldn't have occurred to him that he was squaring off to someone twice his age, half a metre taller and a lot stronger. If the guy wanted to get heavy . . .

'I bet you wouldn't refuse a can of something either, right?'

Ah, bribery, thought Chris. That's more like it. It's like the guy has known Nicky all his life.

Nicky shrugged, which the biker decided meant the dispute was over. He restarted the stalled bike and lifted it back upright with practised ease.

'We're just on the common up ahead. Two minutes, tops.'

He roared off. The boys turned away from the choking smoke and the blinding dust, their ears ringing with the shattering squeal as the engine's revs climbed.

When they could finally see and hear once more, they looked along the lane and saw the bike vanishing up ahead, having turned into a gateway.

'Uh . . .' said Jazz, doubtfully.

Nicky turned to face Chris, all trace of his anger (not to mention his earlier bad mood) vanished. 'What do you reckon? Think they're something to do with the fair?'

Chris doubted it, but remained silent. Nothing was going to stop Nicky checking it out.

'He said "we",' Mac said, thinking out loud. 'He said he wanted to get back to his friends.'

'They're probably gypsies,' Robbie volunteered.

Russell screwed his face up. 'Nah — travellers maybe. But they're not real gypsies and I don't think they have anything to do with the fair.'

No-one asked him why he thought that way. Without further discussion, they were starting to drift along the lane towards the gateway. Chris brought up the rear, his mind fixed on a different mystery altogether.

'What happened to his mate?' he wondered.

Horton's Meadow sounded as if it should be a lovely place, full of old, tall trees, long grass and bright flowers. Perhaps a brook or a lake full of fish. In the imagination, there were scores of cuddly animals — hedgehogs and squirrels, maybe even deer.

The reality was a bit of a let-down. Whoever Horton was, he must have been a loser to have ended up with a meadow like this named after him.

It was quite a large, triangular area, bounded on one side by a strip of green farmland, on the second side by an embankment where the railway used to run, and along the third by a deep, wide drainage ditch and some serious hedgerow. The longest side was almost a kilometre long.

It was mostly flat, except for a double hump in one corner and a sort of gully that ran most of the length. A few paths criss-crossed the area, but the rest of the ground was covered with scrubby bushes with spiky leaves, yellow grass and bare, sandy soil. In a couple of places, Chris remembered, there were the foundations and outlines of buildings, particularly over by the railway embankment, which was now a footpath.

That was pretty well the complete list of the attractions. Chris hadn't visited Horton's Meadow very often, even though they only lived a short distance away. One look and he remembered why.

However, someone had decided the meadow was worth a visit. As the boys approached the gateway, they could hear laughter and shouting, men and children together.

There was a grubby old bus parked just inside. Beyond it were other vehicles, all of them the worse for wear, including three motorcycles (two with no wheels). The cars and vans formed a kind of circle, in the middle of which there was a small collection of tents and shelters.

It was hard to tell how many people might be living there,

but there were at least eight or nine adults and an equal number of small kids in the tent area, while two guys were playing football further along with four kids of varying ages between seven and fifteen.

'These guys must be the first to arrive for the fair,' whispered Nicky.

'I doubt it,' replied Chris.

The blond biker who had passed them on the lane had just parked his bike. He waved them over. They hesitated for a moment, then climbed over the gate and walked towards the circle of tents. By the time they got close, the man had spoken to a tall woman with black spiky hair, and she had produced a large bottle of cola and some plastic cups which she set down on the bonnet of a rusting old car that might just have been a Ford Escort in a previous life.

'Here,' the blond guy said. 'Get these down you. You must be thirsty after your walk, right?'

It hadn't been so far, but none of them turned down the drinks anyway. Nicky emptied his cup with one mouthful, and eyed the bottle wondering if he might get any more. The guy took a long gulp from the bottle, then handed it over.

'So, uh, what are you guys doing out this way?' the man asked, before wiping his mouth with the back of his hand.

Nicky's mental processes had got as far as thinking that the great secrecy surrounding the fair could hardly apply to people connected to it. Without any trace of embarrassment, he told the guy they were checking out whether the meadow was the secret location for the Equinox Fair.

The biker looked back at him blankly.

'The what?'

Nicky was about to repeat himself, but stopped. A small smile crept on to his face and he nodded slightly, as if he had just worked out something really important.

Chris knew that Nicky was getting hold of the wrong end of the stick, so he jumped in to ask their host what they were doing there.

The man's infectious, easy smile broadened a little. 'We're just camping out here for a while, you know? We move around all the time, different places, right? So, a friend said this would be a cool place to hang out for a while, said he thought we might get some odd jobs.'

He paused for a moment, noticing that Jazz, Mac and Robbie had their attention fixed on the game of football. Then he looked back at Chris.

'My name's Greg, by the way,' he said. He moved his hand as if he wanted to shake or something, but just as Chris was about to respond, Greg dived into his coat pocket and pulled out a small, green tin. He opened it, and Chris saw it was full of hand-rolled cigarettes, one of which the man took out and stuck between his lips.

As he lit the roll-up, Greg lifted his eyebrows, watching Chris closely. Chris realised that he was waiting for some return introductions.

'I'm Chris; this here is Nicky, that's Russell and . . .'

'You guys play football?'

Without any effort, Greg had managed to spot the second thing that united the six boys. In addition to being from the same school, Chris and the others were into football in a big way. All six of them were regulars in the Spirebrook Comprehensive team – the older five in the senior team, while Robbie James was mostly still involved with the lower school squad.

In addition, Chris, Nicky, Russell and Robbie had just made it into the youth team at Oldcester United. It was just one of those flukes that crop up every now and again, but Spirebrook had suddenly discovered several really good young players all at once. Not just these four – Jazz and Mac played for the unofficial United 'B' team, a local side called the Riverside Colts.

So, when he asked them if they played, Greg saw the boys' faces light up. His smile became even wider.

'You want a game?' he drawled.

Five of them were looking at the others out on the common, sizing them up. Nicky didn't bother.

'Sure,' he said, grinning just as broadly, 'we'll take you on.'

Five

'We don't have time for this,' whispered Chris.

Nicky shrugged, as if to say that he knew that, but his eyes were telling a different story. Even though the six of them were outnumbered, Nicky was sure they would give the strangers a good hiding. He had forgotten about finding secret ways of sneaking into the fair. All he really cared about was showing the outsiders what a hot outfit they were up against.

For all his slight caution, Chris felt the same. There wasn't much to worry about that he could see. Greg was keen at throwing himself into diving tackles, but he didn't like to run around much. Another of the adult men, Rat, missed the ball more often than he made contact. The other men and the teenage boys had little going for them other than their size and weight.

Nicky had appointed himself captain of the team of six – not that there was a lot of organising to do. Russell in goal, Robbie as the last line of defence, and the other four in a tight diamond – Mac at the base, Jazz and Nicky out wide and Chris up front. Chris saw the ten on the other side looking them over, noticing the six's lack of height at the back as well as their lack of numbers. They seemed confident.

That confidence lasted about 30 seconds. From the kick off, the ten pushed up, and Rat hit a long ball across from the right towards Greg. It wasn't a great cross, but it still looked odds on that Greg had to beat Robbie in any challenge in the air.

Boom! Robbie took off from a short run and thumped the ball away with the centre of his forehead. Greg, who had been walking rather than running, was almost knocked to the floor. It wasn't the last cross the ten tried, but it was the last one they put within ten metres of Robbie James.

The loose ball bobbled around for a moment, then Nicky picked it up, nutmegged a flat-faced kid called Peg (as in 'peg leg', Chris decided) and scampered upfield. The surface was extremely dodgy, but he kept the ball under control as if it was tied to his bootlaces. Flying over the rolling ground, skipping over the yellow grass, Nicky arrived at the ten's goal-line so fast only two of their number had got back.

Nicky's cross was hard and flat. The ten were beaten by the sheer speed and accuracy of the pass, and the goalkeeper — one of the younger kids — never moved off his line. Chris found acres of space at the back post, arriving at the perfect moment to meet the ball and guide it down, back across the goal. It dropped just inside Greg's motorbike jacket, which was marking one of the 'posts'.

Chris continued to circle round towards Nicky, high-fiving his mate and banging heads.

'That's not the first time you've done that,' Greg muttered.

'They always celebrate goals that way,' Jazz replied, missing the point.

They got to celebrate a few more over the next twenty minutes. Chris hit a solid volley that almost went through the little goalkeeper; Nicky ran a one-two with Jazz and side-footed a third; Mac picked up a rebound and got a fourth.

The ten looked shell-shocked by the blitz they were suffering. Rat took over in goal to take a breather. The game was threatening to become dangerously one-sided.

However, the six didn't manage to score again in the next ten minutes. This was partly because Nicky was showing off, trying to put the ball through a wide variety of tricks. On the uneven surface, this was the same as giving it away, but Nicky didn't seem to mind.

But the main reason was that the kid who had come out of goal — he looked about eight or nine to Chris — was a decent player, prepared to run all over the 'pitch' in pursuit of the ball. He was small in height and weight, stringy and pale-skinned, but he had natural speed and balance and a deceptive strength in the tackle that caught most of the six by surprise.

Having up-ended Jazz, the kid ran across the back, about fifteen metres in front of his own goal. Chris saw a chance to rob him, but the boy touched the ball over Chris's out-stretched foot, then chased off after it again.

The pursuit brought him out in front of Nicky, who confronted his opponent with a mocking smile on his face, closing the younger boy down quickly. The lad looked up once, bringing the ball under control with the inside of his left foot at the same moment. He dragged the ball back with the sole of his shoe, then spun round 180 degrees, flicking the ball up.

There were guys upfield calling for the pass, but the two players out on the wing were wrapped up in their own private little battle. It was clear that Nicky had decided that he wasn't going to be beaten by someone who looked as if he shopped at the kind of place Oxfam sent their rejects to. It was equally clear that the kid was determined to show Nicky that he was just as tricky with the ball at his feet. Chris thought about going over to help, but like everyone else he wanted to see how things would turn out.

They didn't have to wait long. The boy brought the ball up on to his thigh, flicked it up again to bring it on to his chest, and lined up to lob it to where Greg was waiting further upfield.

Nicky bought the move, although he seemed disappointed that the battle wasn't going to remain one on one. He bent his knees, preparing to charge the ball down.

The kid threw his foot forward as the ball dropped down past his knee, but it was all part of the feint. In a kind of overkill step-over, he pulled his foot over the ball, then switched direction, touching it forward off the outside of his boot. Nicky was still coming down, twisting to look back, wondering where the ball had gone.

The ball hit him on the rump and dropped off to the side, where the kid picked it up and went forward. Nicky landed awkwardly, his feet skidding from under him. The kid had just played the perfect one-two. Off Nicky's backside.

This was even better than the incident on the bridge with the old lady. Chris and Jazz fell to the floor laughing. Further back, the kid went round Mac, taking advantage of the fact that he was howling and pointing with amusement.

Robbie James was the next up, outnumbered by three attackers as the kid raced forward. He wasn't yet so confident of being part of the gang that he was shrieking with laughter like the others, but he grinned broadly as the kid approached. The smile vanished as he realised he could be the next one to look like an idiot.

26

He slid in to make the challenge and felt the ball strike his shin. There was a moment when he had nothing more on his mind than fear about what his mum would say when she saw the state of his clothes, but then he looked behind him and saw the kid still had the ball.

He was stumbling, off-balance after Robbie's solid, energetic challenge, but he hadn't been robbed yet. However, the ball was running away from him, and it was clear he didn't have much energy left to chase it.

Russell was coming off his line, tall, solid and hard. The difference between him and the small, skinny kid couldn't have been greater. As Russell narrowed the angle, he saw the look that came into the boy's eyes, the look that said he'd seen the wide open goal vanish behind Russell's rush as if by magic. Russell stayed on his feet, head up, arms spread, balanced on his toes.

It was one of Russell's strengths as a keeper that he could read a forward's mind, feeling instinctively when the guy would strike and which way. He knew the boy would decide to shoot early, and he started to throw himself to his left almost as soon as the kid let fly.

He'd guessed perfectly. The only mistake he made was that he didn't expect the ball to come at him so fast. The kid might look like he was held together by string, but he packed a dig in his right foot that wasn't much weaker than Chris's. As he saw the flight of the ball, Russell had only a split-second to throw his hands up to parry it, and even then the ball hit his upper wrist rather than his palms.

The ball flew up and to Russell's right. He twisted his head and breathed a sigh of relief as he saw the ball arc away past the far post. There wasn't much in it, but it had gone wide.

The kid had beaten all six of them and almost scored a blinding goal. Russell looked round to the front once more, ready to congratulate his opponent.

'Goal!!' the kid yelled.

Russell picked himself off the floor (it had been a rough landing, but Russell had taught himself to play in goal on worse playing surfaces than this).

'Almost,' he said, 'but it was the wrong side of the post.'

The kid looked at him, and Russell was shocked at the fury in his eyes. The boy had long, wild, darkish hair, with just a hint of red. It spilled across his forehead, throwing shadows over his eyes, which seemed to shine out of the darkness like torches. They were as bright as sapphires. Russell looked back, blinked and continued to rise.

'No, really,' he began.

'You cheat!' the boy spat, and there was a lot of venom in his voice. Russell almost couldn't reply.

Greg was walking over slowly, hands extended. 'Whoa, hold on, Kim,' he said, 'calm down.'

'It was a goal!' the boy raged. His face was starting to turn red. 'You saw it!!!'

Greg rocked his head from side to side. 'Well, I'm not sure I did,' he said quietly, his accent making him seem quite casual. 'It was a brilliant run and a great shot, but from where I was I couldn't say what side of the post it fell . . .'

'It was in!' the boy yelled, his voice even more shrill.

Russell didn't mind losing. He just couldn't tolerate anyone scoring against him. The defenders he played with at Spirebrook Comprehensive and Oldcester United knew you couldn't afford to give anything less than 100 per cent when Russell was between the sticks behind you.

He opened his mouth, ready to deny the goal again. Then he saw Chris trotting towards him, grimacing slightly and gesturing for Russell to keep calm and quiet.

'Actually, from where I was standing, it did look like it might have gone in off the post,' Chris said.

'It was a goal!' the kid yelled. No-one rose to the bait.

'You think so?' asked Greg, facing Chris.

'Yeah. I think we all know how good it was.'

Greg nodded and went over to slap Kim on the shoulder and guide him back to the ten's half. Chris watched them go and took a deep breath.

'This the new team policy, Chris?' muttered Russell from behind him. 'Are we going to call it a goal if it gets close enough and the striker makes enough noise about it?'

Chris faced his keeper and gave him a consoling grin. 'It always works for Nicky. Anyway, it's four-one, Russell. The kid's – what? – eight? I think we can let him have that one.'

'Besides,' giggled Mac, who was coming back towards them, 'it deserved a goal just for what he did to Nicky.' He stopped when he looked up at Russell and saw Jones wasn't joining in.

'Yeah, great.'

Chris stepped closer and slapped Russell on the arm. 'Come on, it's no big deal. Forget it.' He paused to see if his words were having any effect. 'You've got to admit, Russ, the brat plays pretty good football.'

Russell wasn't prepared to admit anything of the kind. Whatever respect he had developed for the boy at the start of the run had vanished by the end. All the same, he could see it wasn't worth fighting over.

'Fine,' he said. He turned to Mac: 'If he tries it again, clatter him.'

'That seems fair,' Mac said, grinning. He started to move off after the ball.

'I'll get it,' said Russell, turning quickly and breaking into a run. The ball had landed a good 30 metres past the 'goal', nestling under the wheel arch of the mutilated Escort; it would give Russell more time to calm down if he fetched it himself.

'He'll be OK,' said Mac.

Chris nodded, then looked at his watch. 'We'd better pack this in soon anyway. We've got to get back into town.'

Having jogged the first fifteen metres, Russell slowed to a walk almost immediately after. He knew it was silly to get into an argument with a nine-year-old over a disputed goal. The kid looked so winded after that run (not to mention the fact that the six were properly wised-up about him now) that he'd never be able to repeat it. And the guys were still capable of stepping up the pace again and banging in another five or six without getting short of breath.

'It wasn't a goal,' Russell said, low enough that no-one back on the pitch could have heard him, but loud enough to get it out of his system.

He was close to the car's front wing now. He was bending to pick up the ball when he heard the voice.

'You're right,' it said, 'you were too good for that shot.'

Russell froze. All he could see of the speaker was a pair of boots on the far side of the car. But he didn't need to see any more.

'Didn't I always say you'd make a fine goalkeeper, Russo? Didn't I always say that?'

Six

⚽

The game came to an end in sudden confusion.

Having taken several moments to retrieve a ball that Chris could see plainly from almost 50 metres away, Russell returned looking pale and unsettled. At first Chris thought he was still upset about the goal, but then Russell explained he was feeling unwell. At once he picked up his coat from the floor and started to run towards the gate.

'Hey!' yelled Chris, still caught off-balance. 'Wait up!!'

'I'll go after him,' said Mac, setting off. That struck Chris as a good idea. Mac was probably the closest to Russell of any of them. Besides, Mac was the only one who didn't have to retrieve a jacket or something. Mac had actually played the whole game in his sweater.

'What's the problem?' asked Nicky, coming up quickly.

'Who knows?' Chris admitted to his team mate. 'Russell says he's feeling sick or something.'

Nicky's forehead creased into a deep frown. 'Yeah, sure. He's probably still got the hump over that dodgy goal. I don't know which of them is the bigger kid.' He indicated the dark-haired boy with a jerk of his thumb.

Chris didn't comment that it was a bit rich for Nicky to criticise anyone for protesting a bad decision (or claiming a 'dodgy' goal, for that matter). He was quite worried about what had turned Russell off that quickly.

Mac was passing through the gate. The rest of the six – now four – looked at each other.

'He'll be lucky to catch Russell up,' Nicky mocked. 'Jones can run like that for hours.' He wasn't telling the rest of them anything new – stories of Russell's running stamina were legendary at Spirebrook Comp. When he had joined the Riverside Colts, he had routinely run from his house to the

30

training ground and back (including the terrifying river crossing on the oil pipe) twice a week. In the very beginning, he had even run to a few of the away games.

Once Mac was out of sight, there really wasn't much to look at – which reduced the four to looking at each other, completely stuck for ideas.

'Is that it?' asked Jazz.

It looked like it. While Chris tried to get his head round what had happened, Greg wandered over.

'Your mate OK?' he asked. Chris saw that his smile was only slightly reduced, as if the grin was fixed in almost all circumstances.

'We're not sure. Maybe. I think we should be going too.'

Greg didn't seem at all put out by the abandonment of the game, even though this left his mob 4–1 behind.

'You sure?'

'Yeah, we have to be in town in a couple of hours. We've got training.' The realisation Russell was supposed to be going with them hit him even as he said the words.

'Damn!'

'Problem?'

'No,' said Chris, 'I'm sure it's fine. We'd better go, though.' He stretched out his hand. 'Thanks for the game.'

Greg looked both surprised and amused at Chris's formality. All the same he shook Chris's hand, then proceeded to do the same with the other three. Chris worked his way round the rest of the opposition as he collected his jacket. The last one he saw was the kid, Kim.

'Thanks,' said Chris. The kid eyed his hand as if it was a viper and said nothing. 'You're quite a player,' Chris added, then he turned away. He had managed three steps when he realised he couldn't leave it at that. He turned, and saw Kim was still watching him closely. 'It wasn't a goal, though.'

The boy showed what he thought of Chris's opinion with a rude gesture and at least three words which would have earned Chris a grounding for a month. Kim waited for a fraction of a second, then raced away to where the Escort was parked.

'Fine,' muttered Chris, though he was curiously annoyed by the kid's attitude. Still, what did it matter to him?

Greg was waiting by the gate as they went past. 'I could give you a lift, if you need to catch your mate,' he offered.

'Russell knows where he has to be,' Chris replied, having pictured himself on the back of the Suzuki for a moment (something that would have earned him an even longer grounding!).

'Listen, we'll be around here for a while,' Greg said as Chris went past. 'If you want a rematch, come on back.'

Chris nodded to indicate that maybe that's just what they would do, then he and the others broke into a trot as they set off along the lane.

They caught up with Mac at the end of the lane, where it joined the main road. He was breathing hard, as if he had run from Horton's Meadow at full speed.

'Have you seen him?' asked Nicky, who then looked annoyed when Mac couldn't answer immediately. The other four had taken the journey at a much steadier pace, and were breathing a little harder than normal as well, but Nicky was impatient for news.

'No . . .' Mac said after another moment.

'What? He's not Superman. Couldn't you keep up?'

Mac glared at Nicky. 'I did my best! I had him in sight as we came round the bend, but by the time I came on to this stretch, I'd lost him. He must have gone through the hedge and on to the fields somewhere . . .'

That made perfect sense to Chris. Russell knew his way round this side of the river and could have ducked off the track while he wasn't in sight. The odds were he had headed home. That was easy to understand. What Chris couldn't figure out was why Russell had left in the first place.

Nicky looked at his watch with an anxious expression on his face. 'You think he's gone home?' he asked. When Chris nodded, he added: 'I'm not sure we've got time to follow him.'

That was true. They still had to get back to Nicky's, get some lunch inside them and then rush to Star Park. Even with a lift from Nicky's uncle, they were cutting it fine.

However, not everyone was under such time pressure.

Mac knew at once that Chris was looking at him. 'Yes, I know,' he said wearily. 'I'll go. But what do I do when I catch up to him? Should I send him to Nicky's?'

Clearly, none of them was buying the 'feeling ill' story.

'I guess,' said Chris, 'he can reach us at Nicky's place up until about one, then at the club later.'

Mac nodded and then looked across at Jazz. 'Have you got time to come with me?' he asked.

Jazz had that sick, guilty look that he only wore when he was about to defy his strict father. All the same, he didn't want to leave Mac in the lurch.

There wasn't much more to say. The two groups split up; Jazz and Mac heading down the track hoping they didn't get lost; Chris, Nicky and Robbie setting off towards the bridge.

'Sean will go spare if Russell misses training,' muttered Nicky as they went back over the river. It seemed a fair prediction.

'He'll show up,' said Chris. 'After all, he has plenty of time.' Which goes to prove how good he was at telling the future.

In fact, it was a silly prediction from the start. As they set off back into Spirebrook, the three of them knew Russell could still easily get to practice. He was capable of running all day, and Spirebrook was only about ten miles from Star Park. And there were such things as buses.

All the same, by the time they had been to Nicky's house and enjoyed a 'light' Fiorentini lunch of pasta and salad, served up in quantities that would kill a horse, things were getting tight. They hadn't heard from Mac, but perhaps that wasn't so surprising, given that there was no phone at Russell's house.

After picking up their gear and driving across town, the boys were convinced that Russell would be there before them, slightly out of breath maybe from having run the whole way, but otherwise fine. After all, they knew what being part of the Oldcester United youth team meant to him. They felt the same themselves.

But perhaps, thought Chris, it meant even more to Russell. The Jones family were an odd bunch. Russell's dad was a lazy, good-for-nothing; his mother never left the house. In fact, even the garden (if that was the right word for the scrapyard at the back of the battered cottage) was alien territory to her. Davey and Marie, Russell's younger brother and sister, were both dreamers, who had been going to Spirebrook

Comprehensive for the last year, but who still managed to seem invisible there.

Before Russell got on to United's youth training scheme, the family's only asset had been the oldest son, Mick. Sadly, though, Mick was a thief, and a nasty bit of work as well. No-one talked about it any more, but he had tried to get Russell involved in his criminal activities before the younger Jones had talked his way into getting a trial with Riverside Colts.

Mick had been arrested, and no-one talked too much about that either. He had taken stuff from Sean Priest, the Colts, shops on the new retail park and just about everyone else whose path he crossed. Chris had stumbled on to Mick when Mick stole a car from Iain Walsh, the Colts' manager. It had all gone very nasty soon after, and Chris had been kidnapped and tied up in a cupboard for several days.

It all seemed a long time ago now. In fact, these days Russell was just another one of the guys, his past forgotten. After just one season with the Colts, Russell had stepped up to join United, and everyone agreed there wasn't a better shot-stopper in any team they had ever played against.

Chris and Nicky were fanatical about playing for United. But Russell's hunger was different. He'd come a long way to be a part of the new United football school. It seemed impossible that he'd do anything to muck it up.

As Uncle Fabian eased his Mercedes into a narrow space, Chris was still wondering if Russell would be there. It was so hard to get Russell to talk sometimes — and even harder to get inside his mind. If only they had more time.

The trouble was, there was never enough time. Some days, Chris woke up and there didn't seem to be a minute when he could sit back and relax. Chores, school work and homework were always waiting to ambush him.

He didn't normally mind. The hours and days flew by, but that was OK. The reason Chris was always struggling to find time to study or do his share of keeping the Stephens' house in moderate disorder was simple. In his world, football came first. And second. And in the four play-off places.

Some time, when he was little, Chris had started kicking a ball, and now he couldn't stop. Luckily, he was good at it. Tall, naturally springy, well balanced and talented, Chris had played football at his primary school, and then walked into the team in his first year at Spirebrook Comprehensive. Each year, he had scored more and more goals as he became taller, faster and stronger. In his last but one year in the lower school team, Spirebrook had been almost unbeatable (which was in part due to the influence of Nicky, Jazz, Mac and one or two others as well, of course, but it did seem that Chris had been the centre of everything that had happened).

And now, he had achieved the first of the more important goals he had set himself. He had come through the trials to get into the Oldcester United youth squad. All his hard work had paid off – and the reward was even more hard work!

Every night after school – with the exception of Monday, which was for cramming in as much homework as possible – there was training or actual matches. Tuesdays and Wednesdays belonged to Spirebrook; Thursdays and Fridays to United. Then there were Saturdays.

There were two kinds of Saturdays: home and away. When Oldcester were at home, youth squad training took place in the morning at the London Road training centre, a few miles out of the city. After the practice, a bus ran the boys back to Star Park where they acted as ball boys, boot cleaners, sweepers-up and general dogsbodies in exchange for seeing the game for free.

Every other Saturday, training started later in the day, just after lunch, and it took place out on the Star Park pitch or in the United gymnasium.

Finally, between 11am and 4pm on Sundays, there were matches for United against other youth teams from around the country.

The weeks were as regular as clockwork. Chris had got used to the physical demands – the training at United was the toughest he had ever known – but the demands on his time were something he was still coming to terms with.

Collecting his kit from the boot of Uncle Fabian's car, Chris wondered if all the hard work was getting too much for Russell. After all, he didn't have a lot of support at home.

Chris hefted his bag on to his shoulder and turned to Nicky. 'We've got to give Russell more support,' he said instantly, forgetting that Nicky hadn't been involved in his thinking.

Nicky looked around, as if he thought Chris had spotted Jones somewhere close by.

35

Chris tried to collect his thoughts so that he could make sense to Nicky. 'Homework and stuff, you know. He missed a lot of school before he came to Spirebrook. He seemed to catch up OK, but perhaps it's getting on top of him.'

'You think we should help Russell with school work?' Nicky asked in amazement. He flicked his hair away from his eyes. After a moment, his face split into its usual wide, white grin. 'You want to hold him back?'

Nicky had a point. There were some subjects – languages, for instance, where any assistance Chris and Nicky offered would probably see Russell drop a few grades in the exams. He had a mental flash of Nicky trying to explain geography. Nicky, who could get lost looking at a map of his own street.

'I wasn't thinking of just us,' said Chris, hurriedly widening the net of those he intended to bring into his new scheme. 'Mac gets good grades in all kinds of subjects, and Robbie does pretty good in maths and English, don't you?'

Robbie came out from under the boot lid, almost braining himself as he did so. 'What was that?' he asked.

'That's no use,' Nicky insisted, ignoring the younger player, 'they're both in lower years.'

A second good point. Chris really wasn't used to Nicky being so logical – it threw him off balance.

'OK,' he said slowly, stalling for time, 'but there's Jazz – he's good at science and stuff, and you and I aren't that bad at history . . .' He dried up, knowing it sounded a little thin.

Nicky had turned away for a brief word with Uncle Fabian, who was easing himself back inside the Mercedes. The boys started to make their way towards the entrance, spying some of the other members of the youth squad.

'What makes you think Russell's problem is homework anyway?' Nicky demanded as they reached the door. 'He just said he was feeling crook.'

A sick choice of words, in Chris's opinion. All the same, he figured maybe Nicky was right (again!) and that he was jumping the gun. Maybe they could just talk to Russell, or maybe he'd turn up and nothing would need to be –

'No, the way I figure it, something spooked Russell over at Horton's Meadow,' Nicky said, having continued while Chris was thinking. 'He saw something, or heard something . . . and he didn't want to let on that he had.'

'Such as?' asked Chris.

'It'll be something to do with the fair,' Nicky said, tapping the side of his nose with one finger. 'I bet it is going to be at Horton's Meadow after all.'

Chris shook his head and followed Nicky into the door at the bottom of the Easter Road Stand, where one of the training staff was waiting to let them in. He sighed as they reached the passage leading to the changing rooms, then allowed himself to smile. Perhaps he wasn't going to have to get used to Nicky being right all the time after all.

Seven

⚽

Sean Priest was bursting with energy. Certainly the boys couldn't remember the last time he had done so much running during one of the training sessions.

The bad news was that this meant he expected them to work just as hard. The circuit training had been painful; the ball work was torture; the skill training almost killed them!

Now they were playing six-a-side on different quarters of the Star Park pitch, and Sean was racing from game to game, yelling instructions, making substitutions and urging everyone to work harder. On several occasions, he brought himself on as sub, which was a rude surprise for anyone he tackled.

Right now, he was watching the game Nicky and Chris were playing in, and noticing they were having it far too easy against Frasier Gillespie, the other goalkeeper in their age group. As they had feared, Russell hadn't showed up, but their missing friend was a long way from their minds after three hours of hard work. They were enjoying a few moments of calm, having quickly put two goals past Gillespie — one a classic Fiorentini-Stephens combination, the other an outrageous chip by Nicky that had left Gillespie utterly stranded.

They heard Sean order Frasier to rotate round to one of the other pitches. Next moment, the tall, powerful head coach was stripping off his track suit and taking his place in goal.

'Perfect,' said Nicky sourly. He had been in trouble for not taking the practice seriously already, after chasing off after a throw-in and heading the ball in one of the other games.

'Just don't try anything fancy,' Chris cautioned his team mate. 'Keep doing what we were doing before.'

Nicky was all in favour of that. It was a policy at these United training sessions that whoever scored the jammiest goal or made the flashiest play got to collect all the training balls at the end of the session. Nicky seemed to win that honour three times in every four.

Their opponents restarted the game. Chris's team were quickly back in possession after a poor pass out of defence. Once again, the ball went out wide. Nicky feinted to go outside Christian Fox, then came into the middle of the pitch, flicking a sweet pass off the outside of his favoured right foot. Chris accelerated forward behind the last defender to meet the pass. He let the ball run past him a fraction, checked his position and let fly. The ball hit the back of the net just inside the near post with Sean comfortably beaten.

'No goal,' Priest yelled, 'you were too far out.'

They were playing a version of the five-a-side rules, with a shooting area roughly marked out on the pitch about ten metres from goal. The lines had been marked out with a sprinkling of white chalk dust which had quickly blown away. All the same, Chris could have sworn he was inside the area.

Priest caught him measuring the distance in his mind. 'I want you to come in closer next time,' he said crisply. Chris nodded to show that he understood, then retreated.

The coach hadn't finished the reshuffle yet. 'Christian! Go and swap with Adrian.' He pointed over to where a clump of players were waiting for their chance to be brought into one of the four games. Nicky winced slightly as he saw Adrian Greaves stand up and jog over. He was among the best players in the Under-16s group, a left back with a solid tackle and bags of energy. After a word from Priest, he went over to Nicky and marked him closely.

'OK, let's start again!' yelled Priest.

He rolled the ball out to one of his defenders, calling instructions and encouragement as his team tried to push up against the pretty solid midfield behind Chris. Not for the first time, the move broke down quickly. With his back to goal, Chris watched as Kingston Davies brought the ball forward. The long-legged central defender looked out towards the right, but he was cautious of putting the ball out to Nicky while Greaves was all over him.

Chris signalled for the ball to be played directly to him, and for Davies to push up for the return. Immediately, he heard Sean shouting behind him.

'Go right, Daffy! Go right!!!'

Nicky had made a dart into space, retreating towards his own half. Hearing Priest's call, Kingston immediately hit a pass out to the winger.

Chris watched for a moment, then sprinted into the space Nicky and Greaves had left behind them. He could only hope Nicky had enough time and space. The ball was coming straight to the winger's feet, forcing him to stop. Greaves was closing the gap very quickly.

Without a moment's hesitation, Nicky let the ball run through his legs, deflecting it just slightly so that it would run down the line. He started to spin round on the spot, but he never made it. Greaves came into his back hard.

'Play on!' yelled Priest, even before Nicky hit the floor. Chris muttered under his breath and stretched for the ball.

'Street' was the only defender left. Nicky's deft touch had caught the defender by surprise, so Chris knocked the ball a little further on and turned at pace. Sure enough, he saw Downing trying to turn as well, his boots skidding through the grass. Chris corrected the ball's path with another touch, and aimed for goal. 'Street' tried to reach him, but Chris went over his outstretched leg. Not for the first time, he was one on one on goal.

He thought he saw a trace of the line marking the shooting area just ahead, but he ignored it. Priest had come a few steps off his line, perfectly placed to cut down the angle. Chris feinted as if he was going to shoot with his left, but the coach didn't buy it. The gap between them closed.

Priest wasn't as agile as some of the guys who kept goal in the youth squad (Russell made them all look slow), but he was big and he had just enough skill to make life awkward. He stayed upright until the last moment, when Chris was only a few steps away. He dived at the striker's feet, sprawling with his feet to the right and his hands to the left.

Chris had almost left it too late, but he saw the movement Priest made before he dived and reacted instantly. He stabbed at the ball with his right foot, squeezing it under Sean's body and in at the near post.

All that left was the tricky job of keeping clear of Priest's body as the coach threatened to sweep his legs from underneath him. Chris managed a weak hop off his left foot that just about took him clear, but he stumbled on landing and sprawled awkwardly on to the ground.

'Better,' said Priest briskly, without a trace of a smile. He offered his hand to haul Chris back to his feet. 'OK, off you go. Get Rory to come on in your place, would you?'

Chris trotted wearily to the sidelines. The fall had rattled him a little, but he was fine after a few moments. He looked up to see that Nicky was coming off as well, limping a little sorely after the challenge from Greavesy.

'Remind me to take up a safe sport, like white-water rafting,' Nicky said as he sat down. He peeled down one sock and looked at the back of his calf. The skin looked red and tender. 'Did you know Greavesy almost signed for Everton?' he asked Chris after he had inspected the damage. 'Makes you glad he's on our side, doesn't it?'

'You want to worry about the guy Everton thought was better,' laughed Chris, but his heart wasn't in it.

They stretched out their tired limbs and waited to see if they would be asked to come on again. Just before the final whistle, Nicky was called on to take a free kick in the game involving the younger players, but that was the last action for either of them on the day.

Everyone looked physically shattered. The coaches rounded up the last few stragglers and herded them over to the Easter Road Stand, where they collapsed into the seats nearest the touchline, taking on liquid and recovering their breath.

Priest compared notes with the other coaches. Chris saw 'The Terminator', one of the hardest and most demanding members of the team, look up at him twice while he was looking over Priest's shoulder. A small tingle started in the pit of Chris's stomach.

'OK,' Priest called at last, straightening and holding the metal clipboard behind his back, as if there was something on there to hide. 'Good session today. You've all come on well since the start of the season, but — as you can see — it's always possible to work a little harder.'

'It can get worse than this?' muttered Nicky.

'Yes, Mr Fiorentini,' Priest replied (he must have been waiting for Nicky to make that remark), 'it can get a lot tougher. If you want to play against the best, if you want to beat the best . . .' He paused for dramatic effect. '. . . if you want to *be* the best, you've got to be faster, stronger, fitter. And that means training harder. And don't think that means we aren't going to be working even more on skills training.'

Nicky wasn't the only one groaning after that.

'Because of this, I have some news about tomorrow's trip to Stamford Bridge. As you know, Ruud and I have been mates since I played in Holland, and I know Chelsea will give us a good day out. Be prepared to meet some very skilful players down there, especially among the younger boys.'

Chris looked along at Robbie James. His school mate winked back at him. A warning like that would only make Robbie more determined to play well.

'However, I want a small group of you to miss the trip tomorrow and to stay here for a special training session.'

He looked up. Chris noticed there was a tiny smile on his face, the first time he had seen Priest smile all day. He seemed to be enjoying the stunned silence his words had inflicted on the whole squad. The tingle in Chris's guts grew stronger.

'That's because next week some special guests are coming to join us as part of the Equinox Fair celebrations. I'm sorry about the late notice, but there was a chance it wouldn't come together and I didn't want to disappoint anyone.'

A small buzz of anticipation floated around the group.

Priest's face finally split into a broad grin. 'It'll be on the local TV news by the time you get home; next Sunday, kicking off at one pm, two teams are coming up here from a special training weekend at Lilleshall. And in case you don't know what happens at Lilleshall, let me remind you that it's the FA's National Coaching Centre.'

The buzz turned into a partially strangled gasp. Every one of the 135 young players present turned to face the guys seated on either side, asking whether they had known anything about this. No-one had. As the tumult died down, Chris corrected himself. Make that 134 players, he thought.

'OK, hush up!' called Priest. 'The England Schoolboys manager is sending up 30 players from their Under-15s squad. So, I've picked two groups of fifteen to face them. One or two are a little old for the players they'll be against, but their coach wants the England boys to have a good workout. OK, here are the players I have selected . . .'

The list of names began. Priest started with the first group of defenders. Chris could see the hopeful expressions of the younger players fade quickly as they realised that every name read out was from the older year groups. Chris noticed Robbie James looking pale and tense as he realised that no player from his year group had been called.

'What do you think?' whispered Nicky, his voice high with excitement.

'I think he's been left out,' Chris replied. He saw his friend was quite puzzled by this remark, then realised Nicky wasn't interested in anyone else. 'Just wait and see,' he added.

Chris turned back to face Robbie. If he had been just a year or two older, surely –

'. . . James,' said Priest. Robbie's face went white with shock. Around him, mates from his year group were slapping him on the back. Robbie James rocked from side to side under the blows as if his body had gone completely limp.

'I knew he'd make it,' said Nicky. 'What do you reckon? Four out of four for the Spirebrook mafia?'

Chris wasn't so sure. There were plenty of good players in the upper age groups. Priest had already said he might pick some of the guys who were in the Under-16s, guys in their last year of youth football before they were either signed to the club or let go. Did that leave much room for Chris and Nicky?

It was taking an awfully long time to read out the list. The older boys were on the edges of their seats as Priest turned over the top page on his clipboard and started to read the names of the second group of fifteen.

'Gillespie, Akele, Kemble, Greaves . . .'

The next few were all from the group above Chris and Nicky's. As soon as he had worked this out, Nicky's face started to fold into a deep frown. In five seconds he went from certain confidence to despair. He leant forward to speak to Chris, but only the first word had been spoken when Priest said:

'. . . Fiorentini . . .'

Nicky's head snapped up like someone had hit him on the chin with a plank. 'Yes, Sean?' he asked automatically.

There was a ripple of laughter among the other boys, and Priest halted before the next name to let the noise die down. He looked across at Nicky, uncertain whether to be amazed or amused at Nicky's reaction.

'I just called your name out, Nicky,' he said at last.

'I know, boss,' said Nicky, with the same nervous smile he wore in class when he was asked the capital of some far-off, mysterious country like Belgium or Ireland. It was clear that he thought Priest had been trying to attract his attention. 'Sorry.'

More laughter. Nicky looked around him, his expression changing from angelic apology to hot temper.

'Nicky, you do know I was reading out the names of the boys I want to clean the toilets next weekend, don't you?'

Nicky's beak flapped like a baby bird's. Words kept leaving his mouth, but none of them were ever completed. He could hear the merriment around him growing louder. Nicky loved to be the centre of attention, but he wasn't enjoying this.

'Me?' he managed at last. 'What for?'

Priest shrugged, as if no-one should ever need a reason to dump on Nicky. He thought about teasing the midfielder for a few moments longer, but it wasn't going to be much sport. 'Never mind, Nicky. If you're awake next Sunday, would you like a game against the England Schools Under-15s instead?'

'Me?' Nicky said again.

Priest shook his head and went back to the clipboard. 'Where was I? Oh, right. Fiorentini . . . Tony Faulkner . . . Black . . . Blackstone . . . Stephens . . .'

Chris felt the tingle in his belly explode like a volcano. He just about managed to avoid leaping from his seat, but he couldn't help himself from punching Nicky on the arm, hard.

'This is great!' he cried. He listened to the last few names. It took him a moment to realise that Russell hadn't been one of them. In fact, Gillespie had been the first name called. Would Sean really pick him in place of Russell?

Someone else had spotted something else. One of the guys missed out said: 'That's only fourteen names, Sean.'

Priest looked up at Mark Thornby, who had a reputation for being the team's Statto. Who else would have thought of counting the names?

'Thank you, Mark. Actually, I want to have a word with someone before I pick the last substitute. In the meantime, that's it. Those are the players who will be facing England in eight days time.'

Chris could barely contain himself. When his father heard the news, he'd be completely made up! He'd telephone every relative the Stephens family could muster, along with most of the neighbours and a few randomly selected from the phone book. Nicky was just as excited. By the time the Fiorentinis had been told, half of Oldcester would be in on the news.

The pair of them changed in record time and made their way towards the exit. Chris was explaining to Nicky that they would have to be careful about how they told the guys at school ('Why should they be jealous?' Nicky asked, 'they already know we're better players than them, otherwise they'd be here instead of us . . .') when a side door opened and Sean Priest poked his head out into the hall.

'I thought I heard you two,' he said. 'In here, would you?'

'In here' actually meant along a passage, through a set of fire doors, along another corridor, up several flights of stairs and through another three doors. Until the new School of Excellence was finished, Priest's office was hidden somewhere up in the clouds above the Easter Road Stand.

'He heard us from all the way up here?' asked Nicky.

Finally, they arrived in the small office Priest called home. Actually, he even had to share that with The Terminator, who took up a lot more room than a normal-sized human being. Priest's desk was almost backed up against a chart-covered wall, and he had to squeeze round the side before he could get into his squeaky swivel chair.

'Take a seat,' he said. The boys hesitated before deciding he meant one each. They hadn't been into the office since the day, soon after the successful trials, when they had signed the forms that had made them officially part of the United youth team set-up.

A radio on Priest's desk was tuned to Radio 5 Live, though the sound was very low. Chris heard scores and reports coming in from around the Premiership and elsewhere. Liverpool were level with Manchester United; Derby were 2–0 down against Newcastle, with Shearer having hit the woodwork twice as he searched for a hat-trick. Chris thought he heard a scoreline that suggested Sheffield had scored fifteen, but he finally worked out that it was rugby . . .

'How are we doing?' he asked.

Priest didn't smile, and it was obviously not going to be

45

good news. He searched through some papers on his desk, clearly looking for something. 'Two-nil,' he said, without adding any more detail than that.

Oh, well. Leeds were a good side, and Martyn had proved an inspired choice as goalkeeper. Perhaps United's dream start to the season had been too good to last . . .

Priest was now checking the clipboard to see if he had been carrying the piece of paper he was looking for all along. Trying to be helpful, Chris checked the floor.

'Sean, we've been meaning to ask you . . .' Nicky began. Chris sat up quickly, worried about what might be coming next. After all, he had no idea what 'we' had been meaning to say at all.

'What?' asked Priest, irritably. He scratched his chin.

'Do you know anything about who this Portuguese player is? The one United are supposed to be buying?'

Chris could see Friday evening's local paper on the pile of files behind Priest's shoulder. He remembered reading the headline that morning. It seemed a long time ago.

'Unless he's under sixteen years of age, he isn't really my concern, Nicky,' Priest replied flatly. He was clearly preoccupied with whatever it was he had lost.

'Surely you know something about it . . .' Nicky continued, always a poor judge of when to shut up. Priest dropped the stack of letters he was holding and shot Nicky a warning look. To make sure Nicky had got the point, Chris nudged his mate with his knee.

'What?' Nicky complained.

'I'm sure you'll hear, along with everyone else, when there's some news,' Priest said impatiently. At that moment, he caught sight of the corner of a flimsy piece of paper pinned under the monitor of the computer at one end of his desk. His face showed that he remembered putting it there so that he wouldn't lose it. He fetched it out.

'OK,' Priest said. 'Can you guys tell me where Russell is?'

That took a moment to deal with. Chris stared back at the youth team manager, who was peering at them over the top of the flimsy, curling piece of paper. Chris realised it was a fax. He could make out that there were two or three paragraphs written on the other side, underneath some kind of letter head and a large, dark rectangle. It was a pity the paper wasn't just a little more see-through.

'We don't know,' said Nicky quickly. He had weighed up the pros and cons of telling the complete truth and decided to wait. Chris had made the same decision, but he knew his motives were somewhat different.

'You haven't seen him today?'

Nicky took a moment to think this time, pushing his fringe back from his eyes. 'Should we have?' he asked, lamely, a dumb question bearing in mind where they were.

Priest had been involved with Chris and Nicky for a long time. He knew that their first instincts in any situation were to hide the truth from anyone aged fifteen or over, on the basis that they always stood a chance of outsmarting anyone else. Usually, they were right. However, in the last year or two, Priest had been caught up in some of their madcap schemes, and he knew that the best solution in a crisis was to get the truth out of them quickly before they worked out any ideas of their own.

'Let me put it another way,' he said, a new note of patience in his voice. 'Why have I had a telephone message from Donald MacIntyre, saying that I should tell you that Russell has disappeared, that no-one has seen him since the football game this morning, and that he hasn't been home?'

He pulled the yellow Post-It note from the front of the fax paper and waved it in front of Nicky. Chris could see it had the words PHONE MESSAGES printed on the top, and some neat handwriting (not Sean's!) underneath. There wasn't time to see if Sean had given them the whole message. In fact, all Chris could tell for sure was that the Post-It must have been the rectangular shadow he had seen through the flimsy fax paper.

Which was probably not the most important part of the story right now.

'I can explain,' said Nicky, which was a standard opening he used when he had no chance of explaining anything. 'It was just a knock-about, see. In fact, we were just looking to see if Horton's Meadow was going to be used for the Equinox Fair, only there were these guys there, see, camping, and they asked us if we wanted a game . . .'

Nicky dried up when Sean lifted his hand to stop him.

'What are you going on about, Nicky?' he asked.

Nicky looked puzzled. 'The football game?' he asked, no longer sure.

Priest made a small noise in the back of his throat and wrinkled his face as if he had toothache. 'Nicky, I'm not worried about you playing football with some guys someplace, even if it is a practice day.'

Nicky started to make a point; Priest beat him to it.

'I know I told you that the only teams you could play for now that you're with United were this one and your school team, but I didn't mean you couldn't play with your mates. What did you think – that we send guys out spying to make sure you aren't kicking a ball in your back yard?'

That was ridiculous. Nicky's garden had a really high fence.

'The rules just stop you playing for other clubs. It's like Alan Shearer can't play for Newcastle *and* his local social club.'

Nicky considered that for a moment. 'But he can play for England . . .'

'That's right,' said Priest, even though they were straying further and further from the subject at hand. Nicky had this amazing ability to know all there was to know about football – he could name all eleven players plus substitutes for just about any of Oldcester United's home games since 1970 – without understanding one word of his contract with the youth team. Chris knew there were people called idiot savants, basically stupid people who retained incredible amounts of information they could throw back at any time. He was sure Nicky was one, although he wasn't sure about the savant bit.

'Just tell me what happened with Russell,' sighed Priest, turning to Chris for help. Chris gave him the whole story.

'You couldn't have told me this before?' the coach asked when it was over.

That might have been an option they could have considered. 'We weren't sure of the facts,' Chris began.

Priest leant over the desk and pointed at Chris, trying to make sure that his every word was perfectly understood.

'Listen to me, Chris. You've got this really bad habit of needing to be in control of everything. Until *you* understand a problem, you don't share it with anyone.' He flicked his eyes across to Nicky. 'Except maybe with your sidekick, here. Think about it; what happened when Russell first came along?'

Chris could see at once what Priest was driving at. The

youth team manager raised his eyebrows, inviting an answer, but Chris couldn't – or rather, wouldn't – give one.

'And the trouble we had when that American kid came over last Easter . . .'

Chris knew that there were several other examples that could follow. He decided to speak after all, in case he was forced to listen to the whole list.

'This isn't like that,' he insisted.

'Isn't it?' asked Priest, with a small smile on his face. 'What was to stop you coming up to me at the beginning of the session and just saying that Russell wasn't well and wouldn't be coming in today?'

'We weren't sure . . .' Chris began, suspecting this was the answer Priest was expecting.

'Exactly. Russell says he's not well, and you decide there's some great mystery to be solved, and keep it to yourself, when the simplest thing to do is just tell someone what's happening. You're a control freak, Chris.'

There was a short pause while Chris considered what he was being told. Was this the reason why he kept getting into these weird scrapes? Would his life be more peaceful if he allowed the people around him – Sean, his father, teachers at school – to know what was going on from the first moment?

'Hang on a minute,' Nicky said, breaking the silence (which caused Chris to think, Hold on, I'm a control freak? I'm sitting here beside Mr I'm-in-charge Fiorentini, and *I'm* the control freak?). 'What's the big deal, here? So we didn't tell you ourselves that Russell wouldn't be coming – you got a call, didn't you? And so he's missed a session? Is that such a crime?'

There was a moment when Priest was on the edge of giving Nicky a lecture on the importance of commitment, but he held off (for now). That was when Chris suspected there was something more to the story than a simple training session. He knew at once that it was something to do with that fax Priest was holding. It might even explain why the coach had been in such a tense, tetchy mood all day.

The next words Priest spoke clinched it. 'Can I trust you two with a secret?' he asked.

It was a silly question. After all, who ever answers a question like that with 'No'? Priest knew as well as anyone that Chris and Nicky attracted mystery like a pair of magnets. It wasn't that he couldn't trust them not to *tell* anyone the secret, but would the secret survive for long if he shared it with them?

The two boys were leaning forward, eager not to miss a single word. Priest took a deep breath, prayed that he was doing the right thing, and told them what he knew.

'OK. Next Easter, we're opening the new School of Excellence.' That certainly wasn't a secret. The Oldcester United Youth Training School was going to be the first purpose-built, all-inclusive school for young soccer players in England. Instead of the squad members going to one school in the week, and then training with United evenings and weekends, they would be at the new school full-time. There would still be normal lessons (Nicky hadn't escaped from geography) but there would also be even more intensive coaching. The boys (and a small number of girls) would get the kind of sports-centred education kids received in France and Holland. They would study sports medicine, nutrition and other subjects which could help them towards careers in coaching after their playing careers were over.

The new building was going up just along the road from United's Star Park. Already much of it was complete, and the fitting out of the classrooms, gym and training area was taking place. The whole thing had been sponsored by Virgin Cola, the same people who had put their name on United's red and blue striped shirts this season.

Other clubs were following Oldcester's lead. But for a year, maybe more, United would be the only one. It had been Sean's project for over five years, and it was close to completion at last . . .

'We want to have a big celebration when we open the school,' Priest continued. 'So, on top of everything else, I've been trying to organise a special tournament, like the one we had when the Americans were over last Easter. Only I want this to be bigger, with the best youth teams in Europe.'

Chris and Nicky edged even further forward. This was definitely news to them!

'It's been a nightmare to organise. I wanted games for all the different age groups, I wanted to get the girls involved . . .' He looked tired, as if remembering all the letters, phone calls, faxes and meetings. He rubbed his chin. 'Anyway, it's coming together. Ajax are sending over a couple of teams, Manchester United and West Ham have said yes, we might have a team of youngsters from Barcelona or Atletico Madrid, and I heard just the other day that Benfica were interested too.'

The names alone made the boys gape. Which team might they be playing against? Would they get to meet any of the star players from the clubs? When would it all start?

Priest continued, his voice still low and surprisingly flat. How could there be any bad news at the end of this?

'The only trouble is,' the coach continued, 'the building work is running late, and we might not have the school ready before May. I have to spend a lot of time getting things moving or next Easter we'll be celebrating the fact that we *nearly* have the first soccer school in the UK . . .'

'You need us to help?' asked Nicky.

Priest chuckled. 'If I need the Fiorentini family to come out and lay bricks, I'll let you know,' he said. It wasn't such a stupid idea. There were a couple of Fiorentinis in the building trade — two electricians and a plumber that Chris knew about. And Nicky's mum could handle the catering . . .

'No, what I need is for there to be no other distractions. What I need is for you guys to help keep the other stuff running smoothly.'

'We can do that!' Chris volunteered quickly.

'. . . and what I need right now is for you to find out what's troubling Russell and help him sort it out. Because we don't have a lot of time.'

The boys, even though their heads were still buzzing with the news, caught the last sentence and knew it didn't quite make sense. Why was there a time problem?

At long last, Priest waved the fax. As he did so, the top rolled back and revealed that the letter head was the England Schoolboys FA. Was it something to do with the England game, Chris wondered?

It was, but not in the way he expected.

'OK. Try to keep this to yourselves, will you?' He didn't wait to see if the boys agreed. 'Callum McAllister, the guy in charge of selecting the England Under-15s team, sent me this. I was going to let you know during today's session, but . . .'

'Who's Colin McAlpine?' asked Nicky.

'McAllister,' sighed Priest. 'Callum McAllister. He's a teacher

51

at a school in Manchester, but he's also the guy who picks the team for the Schoolboys' internationals . . .'

'A teacher?' asked Nicky. Priest decided not to explain how it all worked just then.

'Take my word for it – he picks the Schoolboys Under-15s team. Anyway, as well as coming over for the game, McAllister wanted to spend Saturday with us.'

'Fancied a night at the Equinox Fair, did he?' asked Nicky.

Priest fixed him with an impatient glare. 'Actually, that's not his main reason for coming, although I'm sure we'll pay it a visit. No, his chief reason for coming is that he's interested in a couple of our players. Even before we fixed up this game for next Sunday, he was thinking of inviting them down to Lilleshall to join the England squad for a training session in December . . .'

Nicky uttered a thin squeal, like tyres on a distant, hot road. Chris felt his heart turn somersaults. Was Priest saying . . .?

The coach must have felt the electricity the boys were discharging. He looked up as if he had been shocked.

'Whoa, slow down,' he said. 'It isn't you two. Not this time.'

Beside him, Chris saw Nicky fall back into his seat. Chris felt a little deflated himself. But the fact remained, two of their team mates were being considered for England schoolboy places! Who were they?

He knew half the answer before Priest said anything. It was the only thing that made sense, the only thing that explained why Sean had summoned them here. And when he heard the second name, Chris knew that made sense too.

52

Eight

⚽

'Russell and Robbie?' muttered Nicky, for what seemed like the tenth time. 'Is there some rule about you can only play for England if your initials are RJ?'

They were almost at the front gate, and Nicky hadn't yet stopped talking. His first words on leaving Sean's office had been to yell: 'Have you invited anyone from AC Milan?' Priest had winced as if Nicky had thumped him in the face. So much for keeping secrets.

Chris had promised Sean that Nicky wouldn't be yelling at the top of his voice by the time they got outside the club, but it was a promise he found hard to keep. He had, at least, managed to change the subject, moving it back to the matter of Russell's selection.

Chris knew why Priest had told them. As soon as Sean told Russell, it would have reached Chris and Nicky next anyway, so all Priest was doing was reversing the order.

'They're the best two players in their positions,' Chris said, generously. Nicky made a sour, mocking face, as if to say that he and Chris were the best two young players in the universe (at least as far as Nicky was concerned). 'Maybe England are already flush with midfield players and strikers,' Chris added. Nicky didn't buy that either.

'Yeah, but honestly . . .' Nicky moaned. 'Look, I've got nothing against either of them . . .'

Chris stiffened. That was a phrase destined to be followed by a 'but'.

'. . . but we don't know anything about James, do we?'

If Chris hadn't known Nicky so well, he could have become very angry on Robbie James's behalf. Instead he knew this was just Nicky's way of coping with being told that someone else was the centre of attention for once.

'Nicky, Robbie was already getting plenty of offers from clubs before he came here. He was on Luton's youth squad before his family moved to Oldcester. Let's face it, he's a better player for his age than anyone we know. And when he's 21 and nearly two metres tall and no-one ever scores another goal against Oldcester again, you'll be the first to remember that we saw him first.'

Nicky thought about that and decided that perhaps he was fighting this particular battle on the wrong ground.

'Maybe you're right,' he said, 'but what about Russell? Look, I know he's a good keeper and all, but two years ago the only people he played against were in his imagination. One minute he's hanging around trying to get a game with the Colts, next minute he gets picked for England? I mean, get real!'

Chris couldn't deny Russell's rise had been meteoric. After one season with the Colts and Spirebrook, he'd got through the trials at United; after less than six months there, he was knocking on the door of England selection. He wondered how McAllister had even heard of Russell Jones in so short a time.

Their conversation was interrupted by the short hoot of a car horn. Along with about a dozen other people still hanging around the club entrance, Chris and Nicky looked around.

'Why do car drivers do that?' Chris asked. 'How are you meant to know who they're honking at?' It was one of his pet hates.

Nicky nodded off to his right to where a metallic grey Mercedes was parked almost in the corner of the car park. Thanks to their meeting with Sean Priest, the boys were late out. Uncle Fabian had waited patiently. Nicky grinned smugly as Chris saw who it was.

'What, and you knew it was for us?' Chris snapped.

'Sure? Who else drives a Mercedes?' Nicky replied.

Chris sighed – who else would have recognised that it was a Mercedes horn?

Just before he was dropped off, Chris exchanged a few last snatches of quiet conversation with Nicky in the back of the car. The Merc's interior was huge, with deep leather seats and faded cloth interior trim. Way up front, Uncle Fabian had asked them how the day had gone, and then settled into concentrating on the busy, late-Saturday-afternoon traffic.

'You're not jealous, are you?' asked Chris in a low whisper.

Nicky looked at his team mate as if Chris had just developed gills, a trunk or green ears. 'Are you stupid? Of course I am!' Nicky snapped. He caught Uncle Fabian glancing at them in the rear view mirror and lowered his voice.

'Don't worry, I don't hate him. I just wish it was me.'

That much Chris could sympathise with. It seemed a long time ago that they had been celebrating getting into the team to face the England Under-15s next weekend. Now they were actually disappointed.

'We better go over there in the morning and tell him the news,' said Chris, aware that this meant missing that evening's *Due South* to get some homework done. Chris thought about taping it, but he already had about six weeks' worth of viewing stored up and he rarely got round to any of it.

'Call for me in the morning,' said Nicky, 'but not too early.'

As if Chris would have dared. Sunday breakfast was the twenty-third most important meal of the week in the Fiorentini house . . .

They had arrived at the end of Chris's road, and Uncle Fabian was turning the big steering wheel to make the slow turn. There was no space to park outside Chris's house, so he pulled up several doors down, near Dr Loenikov's surgery.

Chris waved the Fiorentinis goodbye and turned back along the pavement. He had barely taken a step before he was interrupted by a bush.

'Is that you, Chris?' it asked in a strange accent.

It took Chris a moment or two to realise that the voice belonged to the doctor, an elderly man from the Ukraine who had been living just along from the Stephens' house since — well, since before there had been a Stephens' house. He spoke in a strange mixture of broad Midlands and harsh eastern European, which took quite a bit of getting used to. Dr Loenikov kept threatening to retire back to the Ukraine so he could see how things had changed after independence, but no-one believed he would ever leave.

'Dr Loenikov?' Chris called back, trying to see over the tall hedge at the front of the doctor's garden.

'Down here,' came the reply. Chris realised the voice was much lower than he had first thought, and ducked down so that he could see under the thick leaves. The doctor's lined, sun-darkened face peered back at him through a small gap between two trunks.

'I thought it was you,' Dr Loenikov said, smiling. 'How was training today?'

'Exhausting,' laughed Chris, finding the idea of being bent double, looking under a hedge at a 70-year-old doctor from Kiev a little ridiculous.

'Nothing too taxing I hope. No twinges or pain?'

'Are you trying to drum up business, Dr Loenikov?'

Now it was the Ukrainian's turn to smile. 'Who needs it? This has to be the unhealthiest street in Oldcester. The first drop of rain and thirty people have the flu. You English, you are so pathetic when it comes to bad weather.'

Chris didn't reply. Just because the doctor was as fit as a horse, it didn't follow that everyone in the Ukraine was like that. At the same time, Chris seemed to remember the Ukrainians winning a lot more medals than Great Britain at the Atlanta Olympics.

But then, who hadn't?

'I have a message for you,' the doctor continued. He scratched the end of his nose with one finger. Chris could see he was wearing gardening gloves, and remembered that the lawn on the far side of the hedge was raised up about half a metre. Dr Loenikov was probably kneeling down quite comfortably, weeding or whatever, while Chris was bent over with his head almost at knee level. He considered telling the doctor he would come round to the gate.

'Someone called Jones . . .' Loenikov continued. Chris froze, knowing this could be important.

'What did he say?' asked Chris, impatiently.

Dr Loenikov didn't give him that at first. 'He was here a few hours ago. I guess your father was still at work. I saw him go to your front door, and when he got no answer he walked up and down outside for a minute.'

Chris had no idea that the doctor kept such a close eye on the comings and goings at the Stephens' house.

Loenikov explained why, as if he had read Chris's mind. 'There have been a few burglaries at the far end of the street. I tell you, Chris, this road is not what it was! Some people, they have no sense, leaving their doors unlocked. I have no choice, I

56

must make certain all the drugs and medicines are locked up safely . . .' He was starting to drift, but Chris knew that was just the way the doctor told his stories. The mistake would be to interrupt him, in which case Loenikov was as likely to go back to the beginning as get to the point.

'. . . and I think there are bad people moving into the street,' the elderly man continued, still peering under the hedge at Chris. 'When I saw this Jones outside your house, in his long coat, like a hoodlum in an old movie, I thought it best to check him out. So, I asked him who he was. He said his name was Jones and I was to give you a message.'

Chris listened closely. The fact that Russell had started wearing his old, floor-length coat, the one he used to wear when he went out stealing with his brother, the one he had discarded when he had won his chance to play for the Colts, was a worrying sign.

'Which was?' Chris said, hoping to finally reach the target.

'He said, and I quote: "Tell Chris to keep his nose out of things this time. Tell him the Jones family don't want him poking around in their business. Tell him . . ." and I think I have this last bit correctly . . . "to butt out." '

Chris allowed the words to filter through his mind, digesting them slowly. On one level they were perfectly clear; on another, they just didn't make sense. What was Russell involved in that he would demand Chris stay away?

'Was that it?' he asked.

'Yes,' insisted Dr Loenikov. 'After this, he got on his bike and rode away.'

Bike? What bike? Russell had never owned one. In fact, not a month before, Nicky had been talking about giving Russell his old machine if – as he suspected – he was given a new mountain bike at Christmas. They had made plans to go out into the country, and to use the new cycle lanes being marked out across the city to ride to United for practice.

But in the meantime, when Russell went anywhere, he went on foot. Chris didn't like the sound of this at all.

'Is he a friend of yours, this Jones?' Dr Loenikov asked.

'I hope so,' said Chris.

Nine

—— ⚽ ——

The last thing that united the team mates from Spirebrook, after the fact that they attended the same school and loved football, was that if you said to any of them that they were to keep their noses out of something, it was an open invitation for them to do exactly the opposite. Sean Priest had accused Chris of being a control freak, but that wasn't it at all, at least not in Chris's opinion. After all, you couldn't be an Oldcester United supporter if you wanted life to be predictable.

Oldcester United were the kind of team who had a winning record over the years against Liverpool. True, they had been divisions apart in the eighties when Liverpool were rampant, but the fact remained true. In forty-eight matches between the two teams, Oldcester had won seventeen and lost eleven.

On the other hand, Oldcester had played Darlington three times in the FA Cup, including twice in successive years in the early seventies, and had lost them all without scoring a single goal.

What supporters of Oldcester United learnt from the first kick-off they ever saw was to expect the unexpected. Something of that belief had rubbed off on to the rest of Chris's life. He never expected things to go smoothly. Accidents were always waiting just round the next corner.

And when they happened, you needed your mates round you, which was why Chris never left a mate in the lurch. Whatever Russell's problems were, Chris knew he had to help.

Of course, it helped that he almost had Sean Priest's permission to stick his nose in, despite the lengthy warning about getting too involved. He had a message to deliver. That had to matter more than being told to stay away.

Chris called Nicky as soon as he stepped through the door (which made his father throw his hands up in despair; 'You've just spent all day with him!' Mr Stephens exclaimed). He told his mate what Dr Loenikov had said.

'That's not good,' Nicky said, after he had the story straight.

'That's what I thought,' Chris commented. He could imagine Nicky sitting at home, eyes narrowed, fidgeting with his hair while he considered what they should do next.

'It almost sounds like he's back in his old routine,' Nicky added a moment later.

He didn't need to explain what he meant. 'Hang on,' said Chris, 'let's not jump to conclusions. Just because he's acting strangely –' and wearing his old thief's coat and riding a bike he doesn't own '– doesn't mean he's stealing again.'

Chris knew he'd said all that without sounding very convincing. He wasn't sure what he believed himself. 'Let's just go and see Russell tomorrow, tell him the news about the England game, and see what he has to say.'

Nicky was up for that. 'Should we get Mac and Jazz to come?'

'I think we can handle it ourselves,' Chris said. He doubted Jazz would be allowed out again anyway, and Mac had already told them he was determined to work on his homework. Chris sighed when he remembered this.

'I better go,' he told Nicky. 'I'll have to get my homework finished tonight.'

Nicky laughed, and said how he was going to leave it until Sunday. Chris decided against trying to remind Nicky how much they had to do. Nicky hated talking about work almost as much as he hated doing it.

Come Sunday, Chris was reminded that whatever Nicky's problem with school work was, it wasn't that he was lazy.

Nicky arrived early, having ridden over on his bike even though his place was on the way from Chris's to Russell's, and even though they had agreed Chris would call for him. Nicky had a small green backpack slung over his shoulder. Having accepted Mr Stephens' offer of a cup of tea but turned down toast, Nicky dived into the bag and pulled out a notebook.

Ask Nicky to organise his class notes so that he might be

able to read them, and Fiorentini would ask what was the point. However, whenever Nicky thought he was on the trail of a mystery, he would cover reams of paper with neat handwriting, setting out his thoughts and ideas. Numbers down the side of the page would show each separate piece of evidence, each conclusion and each plan of action. Russell's behaviour being a new subject, Nicky's list only went up to fifteen.

Having been up until past 10.30pm getting the weekend's study out of the way, Chris wasn't that wide awake when Nicky arrived. After listening to twenty minutes of energetic explanations for Russell's behaviour, Chris was even more tired. Yesterday's training really seemed to have caught up with him – and there was more to come this afternoon.

Nicky was still trying to get Chris to offer an opinion as the striker wheeled his bike out of the garage. He waited impatiently while Chris checked the tyres, brakes and gears, and pulled on his helmet and protectors.

'What do you think Russell might be stealing?' Nicky asked as they slipped down the short drive and into the street.

'We don't know Russell is nicking anything!' Chris replied, although the thought came into his mind immediately that he had suspected Russell over the bike.

That seemed to end the discussion for now. Nicky lapsed into silence as they rode along the main road, past the shop Jazz's parents ran, and the bottom of Church Hill. They crossed the bridge, halting at the far end.

As they waited for the distant lights to change and give them a break in the flow of Sunday traffic, Chris looked across the road towards the lane entrance. At first, he wondered again where the Equinox Fair might be held. The narrowness of the lane entrance and the heavy traffic reinforced his certainty that it couldn't be on Horton's Meadow.

Then something else registered in his brain. Something was odd about the view. He couldn't place it at first, only . . .

Nicky was nudging him. 'Hey – look at that!' Nicky said.

Chris looked in the direction Nicky was pointing.

A large red lorry pulling a low-loader was coming slowly over the bridge, preceded by a police car with its blues flashing. The tractor was a powerful German or Swedish model, and it needed to be powerful because it was hauling quite a weight. It was difficult to see what the load might be because it was mostly covered in a dark, dull tarpaulin.

The driver of the police vehicle, seeing Chris and Nicky at the roadside, waved them over the road. After all, he was in no hurry – the monster vehicle was managing a stately 20kph. The boys took advantage of a break in traffic from the other direction to scamper quickly to the far side.

They halted there to watch the low-loader pass by. From side on they had a better view. The huge grey sheet had been pulled over only the front part of the load, some kind of boxy, rectangular shape. Behind it, though, nearly everything else was uncovered.

Long, spidery, metallic arms lay along the length of the loader, folded as if part of a sleeping octopus. They were gaily painted, with rows of light bulbs along their length. Hydraulics snaked from each arm back towards a separate section, which was round and mounted on some kind of motor.

It took no kind of detective to see that it was a fairground ride. The boys could even see its name – THE BUZZ – written in large letters.

'Did you see that?' gasped Nicky, as if there was the slightest chance Chris might have missed the lorry as it crawled past, engine growling angrily at the small cars that whizzed by in the opposite direction. A second police car and a long tail of vehicles snaked back behind the loader, and each driver wore an expression that proved they hadn't missed it either. The Buzz had even managed to catch a bus in its wake, which was almost a miracle on a Sunday.

'You know what this means, don't you?' Nicky pointed out, moving away from stating the obvious now that there was a chance of pointing out who had been right all along.

Chris nodded, trying to avoid looking at Nicky's 'I told you so' smirk. He was leaning back against his bike, watching the low-loader continue down the main road, followed by the train of traffic caught up behind. So, Horton's Meadow had to be the site of the Equinox Fair. He and Nicky (mostly Nicky, he suspected) were going to be the first with the secret – along with four traffic cops and about a hundred bored motorists.

But something else was nagging at Chris, something more immediate. Standing there, he couldn't work it out, but . . .

'We ought to follow it,' said Nicky.

'What for?' asked Chris. 'We know where it's headed.'

Nicky's eyes were alight. He just wanted to be 100 per cent right. Not because he had any doubts at all, but because he knew Chris and the others would have to admit it.

'We have an errand,' Chris said. Nicky's smile faded a little.

'No point standing around here, then,' he said, preparing to mount his bike once more.

That was when it struck Chris. Standing there. They were standing there. Nothing too remarkable about that, only if they had been a bit more tired, they would still have had to stand. There wasn't any choice.

'Hey, look,' said Chris, pointing towards a yellow clump of grass and weeds by the side of the road. 'That's odd. The bench is missing.'

On a scale of one to ten, a missing iron bench – particularly one no-one could sit on anyway because the seat was missing – rated about a minus five on Nicky's scorecard of weird and fascinating mysteries. He took a look at where Chris was pointing and shrugged. 'So?'

So . . . well, so what? Chris couldn't pretend he was having some great insight as a result of seeing the missing bench (or not seeing it, to be strictly accurate), but it was odd.

OK, so it wasn't odd at all. Chris was still struck, though, by the memory that Russell had been sitting on the remaining frame when they had met him on Saturday. The more Chris thought about it, the more he was sure nothing had been wrong then. With either the bench or Russell. However, it wasn't worth wasting much time over it. Nicky was already kicking his pedals round, ready to set off. Chris gave the weeds one last look, then set off along the lane before Nicky left him behind once more.

They took it fairly easily. Neither of them had completely recovered from yesterday's exhausting workout at Star Park. They had more of the same to look forward to after lunch today. No point killing themselves in some race.

They also knew that they weren't going to be able to follow the track for long. To get to Russell's they were going to have to climb a couple of stiles and head off across the fields, following barely marked footpaths. Russell's house was right out in the wilds, with just a narrow farm lane connecting it to the rest of the world. The postmen would have hated it if the Jones family ever got any letters.

Chris believed the reason the cottage was so far from the rest of civilisation was that every other house in Oldcester was ashamed of it. Its out-buildings leant at crazy angles and were filled with junk; the roof was full of holes; and there was a chimney stack up one side of the house which was separated from the main building by a huge crack. It seemed that a decent wind would blow the whole thing over.

There were other houses like it dotted around the area, but they had all been bought by commuters from the city who had had them completely rebuilt and then filled them with fake antique furniture. The first thing anyone who bought one of the cottages did (well, perhaps the second, after getting the drains sorted) was to make repairs to the track that connected the house to the nearest lane (which probably connected to a narrow road eventually).

Not Russell's place, though. Chris had only been there a few times, and Nicky even fewer. Each time, the last few hundred yards had proved harder than the previous miles. After riding along a narrow, overgrown path round the edge of a field, the boys dragged their bikes over a stile into a second field. At the end of that, there was a deep ditch spanned by a couple of rotten planks. That led them on to a farm track which was so deeply rutted that the wheels of the bikes were half under-ground. It was like riding on the surface of the moon.

And this wasn't even the bad bit of road. A narrow turn-off was the final twist in the journey, taking them along a stone-strewn track between thick bramble hedges. The boys dismounted and wheeled their bikes over the stones and rocks.

'Russell does this every morning on his way to school?' moaned Nicky.

'He says there's a slightly shorter way of doing it on foot,' Chris reminded him. Nicky muttered something about broken ankles, but didn't continue the discussion.

The track twisted violently left and right, before finally there was the first sight of the cottage's roof. Just behind it, lay the old railway embankment. The cottage had been built to house the family of one of the people working at the abandoned station just along from there. It was hard to imagine why there would be a station there at all, but old railways were like that. If there were three houses in a clump, they'd call it a village and put a station there.

The nearest real village to Russell's home was West Graves, a tiny hamlet that tried to look scenic but failed. On the other side of the embankment was East Graves, a bigger place by far, and quite pretty. It had roads and everything.

Out here, though, there was just Russell's place, the scrubby fields on which sheep and cattle could be seen grazing, and the barbed wire and bramble bushes. It was very quiet. Every now and again something scurried off into the greenery, but there was no birdsong. When the first bird invented migration, it probably lived somewhere like this.

The boys rounded the last corner. At once Chris stopped. It all seemed unnaturally still.

'What?' asked Nicky.

'That old van of theirs isn't here . . .' said Chris.

Nicky turned back to look at the front of the house. Russell's dad tried to find work (now and again) with the local builders and odd-job men; he even took on jobs himself, whenever someone was stupid enough to look at his hand-written card in a newsagent's window and think they'd found a bargain. He drove a battered pick-up which said Ford on the front, but which was a cobbled together, rusty hulk of unknown make. Its working parts had been salvaged from every type of car under the sun, along with bits from bikes, lawnmowers and probably steam engines too. When the engine was running, it sounded like an Ariane rocket – after it has exploded.

Way, way underneath, the truck was white. However, it carried so much clay and filth, it had a habit of disappearing against a dark background. Chris looked around the narrow yard as if it might be hiding in a corner somewhere. All he could see was the passenger door, which had been propped against the back of the house for months, and a rusty barrel filled with rubbish.

'His dad must be out working,' said Nicky.

'On a Sunday?'

The warning tingle he always got when something didn't seem quite right was buzzing inside him. For a change, he realised what it was right away.

64

'Anyway, his mum would still be here. And crazy Marie.' He had dropped his voice for the last three words, not wishing to cause offence in case anyone was lurking around (such as Marie herself, for instance). Russell's sister was becoming famous at Spirebrook Comp for chalking strange poems on the wall and bringing in vast ropes made out of daisies.

Nicky wasn't tuned into Chris's bad vibes. 'They're probably inside!' he insisted, wheeling his bike across the yard. He leant it carefully against an old table under the kitchen window. The table creaked and something fell off. Nicky moved his bike against the brickwork.

'Hi!' he called through the back door. This was closed, although there was nothing significant about that. It wasn't fixed to the hinges. In fact, it opened on the hinge side, because the lock on the other side was jammed in the frame. No-one had ever been bothered to fix it.

'Hello!!'

Nicky stepped inside.

'Nicky!' hissed Chris, amazed at his friend's gall. He heard Nicky call again, then Fiorentini's head appeared on the other side of the kitchen window, wearing a stupid smile.

Chris followed him as far as the door. By the time he arrived, Nicky had moved on. Chris could hear him in the hall, still asking 'anyone here?'

If there was, they'd have heard Nicky by now. There wasn't another sound around, barring a slight stirring of the trees along the bottom of the embankment. Chris took a long look round the yard. It was just the usual junk, only without the truck in the middle of it. Why did it seem sinister today?

Suddenly, Nicky appeared in the far doorway. His face looked taut and pale. 'You better come see this,' he said.

Chris stepped into the kitchen. It smelled damp, and there was a slight whiff of rotting vegetables from the sink, in which pots and pans were piled high. He stepped past the boxes with a door on top that served as a table, and through the open doorway into the hall.

There was no such thing as tidy in the Jones household, but Chris could tell that the hall was some way beyond the normal state of mess. The staircase alongside was strewn with emptied suitcases, old sheets, moth-eaten clothes, rotting books and other junk. A lot more had landed in the hall itself.

65

Chris took a quick look into the front room, which was in an equal state of chaos.

'What's happened here?' he asked.

Nicky was at the front of the house, close to the main door. Near his left hand, there was another door which appeared to be some kind of small cupboard. It opened towards the foot of the stairs, but there was so much junk piled up against it that it was jammed.

Nicky pulled at a couple of the items, throwing them on to the stuff piled against the front door. After a few moments, Chris joined in too. He had heard the same thing Nicky had.

As they threw the junk aside, the noise grew louder, like a factory siren or a flood warning, muffled by the closet door. As it grew louder, the sound grew higher too, until it was almost shrieking.

Finally, the floor was clear. Nicky took hold of the closet handle and pulled, but still the door didn't open very far. Chris stepped up behind his mate and took hold of the edge. They tugged together, and the door shook as it opened a little wider. It was as if there was a huge weight hanging on the far side.

They gave it one last try, and the door sprang back, slamming against the wall at the foot of the stairs. The dull light from the gloomy hallway crept into the cupboard.

She had been almost dragged out into the hall anyway, her hands fixed on the door's inner handle. Her hair was stuck to her wet cheeks, stained by tears that still welled from her puffy eyes. She shrieked again, then fell silent as she saw Nicky's shocked face looking down at her.

When she looked up at Chris, he saw the bloody bruise above her eye and the angry marks on her upper arm. Marie Jones managed a brief smile, then her pale eyes rolled up in her head and she fell on to her back in a dead faint.

Ten

'Is she OK?' Nicky demanded, sounding really worried.

Chris didn't know what to say. Clearly, Marie wasn't in a good way, but he had no way of telling how bad things might be, and only slightly more idea of what to do to help her.

'We need an ambulance,' Chris said. It struck him at once that there was no phone in the house. 'I'll go,' he added.

Nicky looked up as if Chris was suggesting he should test for gas leaks with a candle. 'You're leaving?' he choked.

'One of us has to, and I think I know the paths Russell uses better than you. I'll find a house with a phone, call for help and then get back here.'

Nicky nodded, although it was clear he'd sooner be the one to leave. 'What do I do?' he asked.

'I don't know!' Chris said, although a few ideas suggested themselves right after. 'Keep her warm!' He found an old, musty blanket amongst the other junk. 'If she wakes up, make sure she drinks something.'

Nicky nodded, and flicked his hair from his face. Almost immediately, he did the same for Marie, more or less, lifting her wet hair from her cheek and smoothing it back behind her head. Chris noticed that the wound over her eye wasn't actually leaking blood at the moment, which he took to be a good sign. Marie looked pale, but that was her normal skin colour, so he couldn't tell much from that.

'I'll be as quick as I can,' he added, then rushed back through the kitchen and out into the yard.

He had no way of telling how much of an emergency this was, but he knew it wouldn't pay to take any chances. It was going to take a long time for an ambulance to get here anyway, so the sooner he got them started the better.

Out in the yard, he started to pick up his bike, then

stopped. Was there any point? He'd only have to wheel it back down the track anyway. And then what? Across the fields and on to the lane and . . .

Too far. The villages were closer. There had to be a quicker way to get to West Graves (a name that filled him with concern, all of a sudden) if he could just work it out.

He looked back past the house. The railway embankment was about ten metres high, strewn with bushes and weeds, but clear on top. Chris recalled Russell saying it was the starting point of his route to school.

Chris knew his route would be the other way. He was equally sure Russell would have rigged some clever way to the top of the embankment. The decision was made. Chris stripped off his cycle helmet and dropped it by his bike. Then he went back past the kitchen, up the short 'garden' at the rear of the house, and through knee-high weeds until he was at the foot of the embankment.

Russell didn't let him down. A worn path up the slope showed where he climbed up, using a length of knotted washing line fastened at the top. The embankment wasn't that steep and Chris soon hauled himself up to the top.

His chief hope had been that he would spot some other landmark from up there, and he wasn't disappointed. On the far side of the embankment, he could see the houses of East Graves about two kilometres away. The grey ribbon of the road that connected it to its sister village wound towards the embankment, disappearing under it about 300 metres away.

Two klicks. Too much? Chris turned round to look the other way. He couldn't see the road from there, except way off in the distance where he could also make out the buildings of the posh private school. Slightly nearer, he could see the village church in West Graves. That looked closer, maybe a kilometre and a half and a little downhill. The village was tiny, but Chris figured there would have to be a telephone.

That was the best bet, he decided, and he started to run along the embankment. The flat top made getting up some speed easy, and he followed the gentle curve round, keeping his eye open for the bridge he expected to see where it crossed the road between the two Graves.

It came up quicker than he expected. One moment the embankment was open on both sides, then there were low brick walls at the edges, almost hidden by weeds. Chris came to a halt and looked over the western edge.

He knew there would have to be a way down – Russell would have found a way to reach the road from here. The problem was Chris couldn't see it. The sides of the embankment were steeper here, and higher too. He considered sliding down on his backside, but he didn't fancy it much.

He checked the drop on the other side of the road. It was no better. Damn! Chris scanned the area again. He wanted to be sure before he took a chance on skidding down.

That was when he realised he could see the bright tents of the small camp on the far side of Horton's Meadow, not much more than another klick away. The old railway continued its slow curve around the edge of the common, slowly dropping down as it did so. From where he stood, Chris could see that the drop to the meadow was less than four or five metres, compared to the twelve or fifteen where he stood.

Would it make sense to go that way? It would be longer – a few hundred metres around the embankment, at least twice that far across the meadow, then along the lane, on to the road and into West Graves from the far side. On the other hand, it was safer. Chris knew he'd be no use to Marie if he fell and broke his leg trying to get down from there.

There might be one other bonus. Greg had a bike.

Chris hovered between the two choices for a moment, staring across the meadow. That was when he saw movement. Someone was skulking along the edge of the meadow on the far side, making best use of the shadows of hedges and a ditch. It was hard to make out much, but Chris was sure the guy was tallish, red-headed and wearing a long coat.

'Russell.'

That clinched it. Chris was going to feel a little guilty later about what had finally prompted the decision (he should have just been fixed on what was best for Marie), but right now it didn't matter. Going the long way round would bring him closer to Russell, and Jones was, after all, the reason they were here in the first place.

Chris took off. He knew that if the sneaky figure in the meadow looked back, he would spot Chris easily against the sky. But he had no way to hide, and speed counted for more than concealment for now.

Even after the distance he had run already, Chris wasn't troubled by putting on some extra pace as he raced along the embankment. All the time, he kept his eyes fixed on Russell. The other boy, hunched low under the shelter of some trees, only vanished from sight when he went round a corner of the irregularly shaped common, and by that time Chris was above the edge of the meadow, and preparing to drop down.

The slope here was much gentler and the embankment was much lower. Without hesitation, Chris spotted, then took, a small, gravel-strewn path down the side of the embankment. His trainers skidded through the loose earth, but he didn't fall. When he hit the bottom, he was still running.

He had to slow a little now, since the common was dotted with rabbit holes and other interesting ways to snap an ankle. However, there were a few clear areas and pathways, and Chris was soon within sight of the tents over by the gate. He could see Greg and Rat loading something on to the group's van. Their voices carried over the common. Rat appeared to be telling Greg that he was doing it all wrong.

From about 30 metres away, Chris called out. Neither Greg or Rat looked up; the first person to see Chris was Kim, the broody kid with the thick, rusty hair and the sullen face. The boy popped his head out from one of the tents, as if he had been waiting for someone to call. When he saw it was 'only' Chris, he frowned deeply and curled his lip in distaste.

At the second attempt, Chris caught Greg's attention. He flew over the last few metres, pulling up just in front of the two men. Rat scratched his head in the space between the clumps of hair that grew along the side. Greg just smiled, as if Chris's yelling was an everyday occurrence.

'There's been an accident!' gasped Chris, and he was about to add: 'I need to use a phone' when he realised he had run out of breath. He bent forward and sucked in lungfuls of air, then straightened up and tried again.

'Do you have . . . a telephone?' Chris asked.

'No!' said Greg, smiling. His eyes were showing some concern even if his lips were stuck in that grin. 'What's this about an accident?'

'We need an ambulance . . . at my friend's house.'

Most adults in situations like this want to hear a complete explanation before they take a kid's word for anything. Fortunately, Greg didn't need to hear any more. He dropped what he was carrying (a pile of scrap metal, mostly thin sheets of tin) and rushed towards his bike.

'There are phones in the village,' he said, jumping into the saddle. He kicked the starter lever and the bike roared into smoky, noisy life. 'Come on! Hop on!!'

Chris hesitated for a moment, looking at the loud, oily machine and its slightly off-the-wall pilot. The idea of the ambulance was to help Marie; he hadn't planned to pre-book one for when he fell off the back of Greg's bike. At the same time, what else had he expected when he came here?

The thought bounced around at the back of his mind that he had come this long way round in the hope that he could catch up with Russell, but that seemed a dumb idea now.

Chris jumped on to the pillion and closed his arms round Greg's waist. Before he could say another word ('Help!' would have been his first choice), the front of the bike lifted up fractionally as Greg throttled the engine, and Chris felt the machine slipping left and right as they skidded over the grass.

Chris had his eyes closed, so he could only imagine that Rat or one of the others had opened the gate, and that they hadn't just gone right through it. He imagined it like a Road Runner cartoon; he and Greg would fall apart like sliced bread as soon as they stopped. He imagined a number of other things too as they blasted along the narrow lane, many of which involved less amusing ways to die. Chris thought they must be doing 100kph, minimum.

Then Greg turned the bike on to the road to West Graves and really fired it up. The noise was deafening. Wind exploded into Chris's face as if he was in the midst of a tornado. His arms felt like they were being torn off at the shoulders.

Moments later, brakes howling like ghosts, the bike came to a stop, travelling the last twenty metres sideways. Chris didn't so much step off as fall off.

He dialled with trembling fingers. Immediately, it seemed, the operator asked which service he required.

'Ambulance . . .' Chris said, snatching at the word. He turned round, and saw Greg was watching through the glass door.

'. . . and police.'

Eleven

The emergency service number is a wonderful thing. You dial 999 and right away all these people are there for you, ready to help you out of whatever jam you're in. It's that simple.

At the same time, it does require the person making the call to have a basic understanding of just what it is they need . . . and where. It was only when Chris was speaking to the operator that he realised just how important that was.

He told the operator that he was calling from a phone box in West Graves. He told her that his mate's sister had been hurt. The first breakdown in communication came when he tried to explain that he and another mate – not the mate whose sister it was, another mate – had found her in a cupboard at the foot of the stairs in the first mate's house.

Quite sensibly, the woman decided she didn't need to know too much about who was 'friends' with whose sister. However, what she did need to know was the address. And that was where Chris was stumped.

'I don't know the address,' he said helplessly. Realising this had to sound odd, he added: 'I just know where it is . . .'

The woman wasn't quite ready to give up just yet. 'Do you know the number of the house?' she asked. No. 'Do you know the road?' No. 'What part of Oldcester?' No.

'It's near West Graves,' Chris added after his third 'no'. 'There's a lane nearby, a farm track. And a railway embankment.' Chris kicked himself. He could just imagine an ambulance, sirens blaring, thundering along the old railway line . . .

'Is there an adult there I could speak with?' the woman asked, her voice sounding strained for the first time.

'Look!' Chris exploded. 'It's an old cottage under the railway embankment, between West and East Graves. It's about half a kilometre from where the road goes under the embankment, facing towards the river. But there has to be another way of getting there, because there's a farm track that goes almost to the front door. Don't you have a map?'

'No,' said the woman, who clearly didn't appreciate Chris's attitude. 'Isn't there a phone at this place?'

'No!'

'OK, who lives there? What name is the house in?'

'Jones,' said Chris. He was sure of that, at least. It was just a pity Russell didn't have a less common name. As he thought about that, he wondered also just how official the Jones family's occupation of the house might be . . .

Chris could hear a whispered conversation at the other end of the line. 'OK, here's what we do,' the woman said. 'Is there anyone with you?' Chris told her that Nicky was still with Marie but that he had someone else with him too. 'Good. Go back to the house. Then one of you go back to the bridge on the embankment, and another follow the farm track to wherever it comes out. The ambulance will look out for you, and you can lead the police and paramedics from there, OK?'

Chris was happy to agree to anything. 'What about Marie?'

'Just keep her warm. If she wakes up, talk to her so she doesn't drift off to sleep again. We'll take care of the rest.'

Chris put down the phone. He was breathing harder than ever. Trying to get the ambulance organised was almost more taxing than running a couple of kilometres. Now all they had to do was get back to the house . . .

'Why did you ask for the police?' asked Greg nervously as Chris stepped out on to the road.

'Pardon?'

Greg looked around both ways quickly, grimacing when he saw that a few of the locals were on their doorsteps, wondering what mayhem and murder had been brought to their village on Greg's foul-smelling machine.

'You said there had been an accident . . .'

Chris looked up. 'Look,' he said. 'I don't think it was just an accident. It looked to me like someone had broken in.'

'It wasn't any of us!' Greg snapped, defensively. Chris wondered why; he hadn't accused Greg of anything. Perhaps the denial actually proved something else . . . After all, Greg had no way of knowing when this thing had happened, and he couldn't have kept track of everyone from the camp. Where, for example, was the guy in the mirrored shades?

'Can we talk about this later?' Chris asked. 'I have to get back so I can meet the ambulance . . .' He stopped, wondering whether Greg would offer to help.

Greg looked even more nervous, which excited Chris's suspicions that there was something going on.

'How do we get to this place?' the biker asked at last, his voice edgy. Chris felt like shouting a small cry of triumph – then he realised Greg was walking back to the bike.

Perhaps another run wouldn't be so bad after all.

It wasn't so bad. Greg took the ride along the Graves Road quite slowly while they looked for the farm track. They went just far enough along it for Chris to be sure they were heading the right way, then turned back so Greg could drop Chris back at the road, ready to flag down the ambulance.

The first sirens sounded a few minutes later. It was the police, and they came along the Graves Road without any hesitation at all. Chris was all ready to wave at them when they swerved past him and on to the farm track.

A second police car arrived a minute later, leading the ambulance. It too turned briskly on to the track, but the paramedics had a little more difficulty. Chris ran towards the police car while the ambulance backed up in the narrow road, ready to make a second attempt at the turn.

'Are you the one who called this in?' asked the driver of the police car, a WPC with red hair and freckles. Chris nodded. 'Get in!' The WPC leant back and threw open the rear door. Chris dived in and hung on to the seatbelts as the car set off down the track at a bumpy 20kph.

The problem of the stone-strewn path up to Russell's house troubled Chris's mind until they arrived at the opening. In fact, Nicky had shown some real initiative. Marie had come round once more, so he had helped her to her feet, out of the house, and on to the saddle of his bike. While she clung on to him and the bike with equal determination, Nicky had gently wheeled it along the track until they reached the farm lane. When Chris arrived, they were sitting by the side of the road at the end of the stony track.

It had saved the ambulance a boney ride and who knew how much time?

The two of them were sitting by the side of the lane, looking very sheepish as they were caught up in the whirlwind of flashing blue lights and sirens. The coppers from the first car went to the house. The second pair stayed with Marie, asking questions she didn't seem able to answer, then quizzing Nicky. The woman with the freckles seemed particularly forceful.

After a while, her partner came over to Chris.

'She all right?' Chris asked.

The policeman, a young guy with dark hair and a vivid red scar along the line of his chin, looked back over his shoulder. Marie was wrapped in a blanket, and the paramedics were checking her blood pressure and pulse, but she looked more startled than injured now.

'She'll be fine,' the policeman replied. 'It's a solid whack on the head, but nothing too bad.'

'Still, I'm glad you got here so quickly,' Chris said emphatically. 'How did you find the way so fast?'

The copper laughed. 'We all know the way to the Jones's house,' he said, with a wink. He touched his chin. 'See this? I got this when we arrested Mick Jones, down at the river.'

Chris looked at the scar. He hadn't been there at the exact moment when Russell's brother had been arrested, mostly because he was locked up in a cupboard at the time (which was rather eerie, bearing in mind where they had found Marie). But he had heard a lot about it from Russell, who had had a bird's-eye view after dropping his brother into the river. Mick had struggled when the police hauled him into the boat, but he hadn't been able to break free.

The copper was looking at Chris closely. 'Come to think of it,' he said, 'don't I know you too?'

Chris offered a shy laugh. Here it comes, he thought. There had been plenty of times in the last year when people had stared at him in the street, or come up to say hello. During the Mick Jones affair, Chris had been missing for a few days before he was rescued; his picture had been in all the papers. Afterwards too, there had been local TV news and lots more press.

Quite a few people knew him through football as well. Chris was quite a celebrity in Spirebrook – not that this was

75

saying much. The only other famous person who lived in the 'Brook was a guy who bred championship-winning hamsters.

'Yeah,' the copper said, his face brightening as he made the connection, 'you're the kid who was involved in that fire at Spirebrook school.'

Chris's heart sank. That was an incident he thought had been cleared up. It was Chris's turn to make a connection. 'You're the ... officer who was on the door, aren't you?' He took a deep breath, glad that he had stopped himself just in time before he referred to the policeman in a less flattering way.

The copper smiled. 'You've got a good memory for faces,' he said. 'You ought to think about being a detective when you're older.'

Chris refrained from remarking that most of his problems came from thinking he was a detective *now*. 'You don't still think I had anything to do with the fire, do you?' he asked, feeling a small surge of panic.

'No,' the officer said, the smile deepening, 'but I know a man who does ...' Chris knew who he meant. There was this big, lard-filled beat copper who had stumbled across Chris and Nicky a few times, and who had decided they were the local equivalent of the Mafia. 'It's just as well he wasn't called out to this,' the young officer said, nodding towards the house. Chris was thinking the same thing.

He looked over towards the others. Nicky and Marie were sitting by the ambulance. The two paramedics had slowed down a lot since their arrival, which suggested that they didn't think Marie's injuries were serious. The taller one with the blond hair and the glasses was actually laughing. 'You fell down the stairs and into the cupboard?' he asked, scratching his head. 'That's stupid!'

His mate didn't find it so funny. He had just worked out they were going to have trouble backing out of the lane again and was yelling at the driver of the second police car to signal directions. She stomped off down the lane.

'Come on, then,' the younger paramedic said, standing up and away from Marie. 'We'll take you to the hospital and get someone to take a look at you.'

Marie looked up at him wide-eyed. The paramedic had no

way of knowing that this was her normal expression and thought she was frightened.

'Want me to carry you?' he asked. His mate glowered at him as if to say that he wouldn't be that helpful to someone who was buried under a ten-ton safe, and that Marie could walk just fine. Eventually, though, he came over and picked up Marie in his arms. 'Strewth – you don't weigh much, do you? I've picked up rugby balls that are heavier than you.'

Chris could imagine it. The guy was big and broad, much the same build as 'Flea', Spirebrook's PE teacher. The thought prompted Chris to speak.

'You play rugby? So does our sports teacher.'

'Yeah? Who's he?'

'Mr Lea . . .'

The paramedic paused at the back of the ambulance. 'Frank Lea? Yeah – we play in the same team. I play centre . . .'

Centre? Chris didn't know much about rugby, but he had always thought the centres were smaller guys, like the wingers. Wasn't Jeremy Guscott a centre?

'Where does Fl – Mr Lea play?'

The paramedic laughed, restlessly stretching his back as if he was day-dreaming about their last game together. Chris was terrified that he might spin-pass Marie into the back of the ambulance. 'He's our scrum half.'

He caught Chris gaping at him in amazement. 'I know, a lot of people think he's too big. That's part of our style, you see. Every bloke in our team is bigger than his opposite number. You should see the guy we have at prop . . .'

He lifted his left hand up and scratched his chin. It was like he'd forgotten he still had Marie in his other paw. 'When the other team come out on to the field at the start of the game and take a look around, and you can *feel* them thinking "Look at the size of them!" And their number nine takes a look at our number nine and decides that he won't hang on to the ball much all day.'

Chris let that thought sink in. He had played plenty of times against teams with older players – it happened when you were much better than kids of your own age. He wondered if there had ever been a time when he had come out, looked at the opposition defence, and decided that it wasn't a good day to hang on to the ball . . .

While he was thinking, and the big paramedic was taking Marie on to the ambulance, Nicky came over.

'Chris,' he hissed, 'you aren't going to believe this . . .'

Chris felt a chill pass over him. 'What?' he asked.

'Marie thinks it was Russell in the house, tearing it apart. She came home, and heard someone upstairs. She caught a glimpse of him from behind, but then she fell, and whacked her head. All she can remember after is that she locked herself in the closet. Russell tried to get her out but –'

'She's sure it was Russ?' choked Chris, horrified.

'I asked the same thing, but that's what she said.'

Chris couldn't believe it, but there was no time to deal with it then. The wiry paramedic had climbed into the driver's seat and was about to reverse back down the lane. Then Chris heard the rugby player call from inside.

'Hang on, Christian!'

He dropped back out on to the lane. 'Which one of you two is Nicky?'

Chris looked round at his mate. Fiorentini was loitering at the side of the lane, trying to keep his bike out of the way.

'She wants you to come with her,' said the paramedic. 'Hop on! The cops will look after your bike.'

The rugby player had no idea what he was asking. Nicky would sooner saw his own head off than go to hospital. Chris suspected that the look of horror Nicky was wearing on his face also had something to do with suddenly being the focus of Marie's attention.

He got into the ambulance like a condemned man on his way to the electric chair. Once the doors were closed, the tall paramedic started to drive the ambulance back down the lane, reversing the big vehicle with some difficulty through the narrow space. Every few metres Chris heard his near-namesake yelling at the WPC guiding them.

'That's stupid! How am I supposed to know that means turn left? Signal properly!!'

The young, dark-haired copper came up and followed Chris's gaze. The ambulance had disappeared, but the sound of the argument between the paramedic and WPC Freckles carried back to them for several minutes.

'Barking mad, those two,' he smiled. Chris offered a grin in return, assuming he meant the two paramedics. 'It's a standing instruction to the Oldcester Police that if one of us gets injured, we'd sooner be driven to Leicester or Leeds, rather than risk being taken to Oldcester City General.'

Chris nodded. 'Are all the paramedics like that?'

'Sure,' said the officer, slipping Chris a sly wink. 'But they're not the problem. Oh, no – if you thought those two were madmen, you should see the doctors!'

Twelve

There was a lot more rushing here and there and a great many more questions, few of which Chris could answer. His mind was filled with what Nicky had told him. After an hour or so, the police had satisfied themselves about two things. The house was empty, and someone had made a lot of mess while they were looking for something.

Chris looked at his watch a few times, knowing that he was going to have to set off for training sooner rather than later. He could just imagine how Sean Priest would take it if instead of turning up with Russell, Chris went missing as well.

'Excuse me,' he said to the dark-haired policeman.

All four of them turned to face him. WPC Freckles wasn't in a good mood – it probably had something to do with the fun she had endured while guiding the ambulance back to the road.

'Just why were you here?' she snapped.

Chris recoiled a little, but then calmed down. After all, he hadn't done anything wrong (had he?); he could explain everything (couldn't he?).

'Nicky and I were here looking for Russell Jones,' he said. He watched the policemen look around at each other, nodding in a 'We all know what *that* means' sort of way.

'We know Jones,' the WPC commented. Chris didn't like the note in her voice. Had Nicky said something?

'Hang on,' Chris said quickly, 'he didn't do this to Marie . . .'

The officer's face twisted mockingly. 'No?' she asked.

'No! He looks out for Marie all the time!'

'I see,' the WPC replied. Chris noticed that she didn't write any of this down in her little notebook. Perhaps he should have added that Russell didn't normally trash his own house, either.

Freckle-face's partner took over. 'Has there been anything

strange happening lately, you know, with the Joneses?'

'Strange?' asked Chris in a choked voice, stalling for time. In his head he had got as far as 'Strange' as in Russell running off and skipping practice; or the fact that all the rest of the family seem to have vanished? Well, now that you mention it . . .

'Well?' the officer asked.

'Not really,' Chris replied, weakly.

Freckles turned away as if Chris had confirmed her suspicions that he was in on the conspiracy. Just what I need, he thought, another friend in the police force . . .

The dark-haired guy looked Chris directly in the eye. 'When was the last time you saw Russell, Chris?'

Chris took a long, deep breath. There was no way he was prepared to lie about that. Wouldn't it make sense for them to speak to Russell and get things sorted out?

At the same time, his dread that Russell might be slipping back into his old ways made Chris pause. He might just be about to point the police directly at his mate. The thought of it made him feel sick.

'Well?'

'Just before I called you,' he said. 'Come on, I'll show you.'

The crew from the first police car agreed to drop off Chris and Nicky's bikes in Spirebrook. Chris gave them Nicky's address – he wasn't prepared to have them turn up at his place.

Meanwhile, Chris got into the back of the second car and prepared for the roundabout journey to the meadow. The police shut up the house as best they could, planning to come back if and when they had spoken to Russell.

Chris sat on the back seat with a growing sense of worry. Was he doing the right thing? All he could be sure of was that he had seen Russell sneaking around the edge of the common. Whatever Nicky might have heard, he was completely convinced that Russell couldn't have done anything that would have led to Marie getting hurt.

So, what did that leave? Chris wasn't sure. All he knew for sure was that there was something nagging at him, needling him. And the answers lay at Horton's Meadow.

He jolted upright. Looking back in the rear view mirror, WPC Freckles saw him.

'What's wrong?' she asked.

'Nothing!' Chris insisted, but he knew she didn't believe that any more than she believed anything else he had said.

Chris couldn't deal with that now. A new thought had popped into his mind and it wasn't going to back down. Chris let it swill around for a while, but he couldn't come up with an answer.

What had happened to Greg?

Five minutes later, the police car pulled up outside the gate on to the common. When they saw the tents and the people camped out in them, the two police officers developed bad cases of wrinkled noses, as if they could smell something.

Greg's friends didn't look any happier to see the police appear. As Chris stepped from the back of the car, he saw Rat looking at him as if he was a traitor or something. The big man shook his head without ever looking away from Chris's eyes. Kim, the frowning brat from the football game, was sitting on the bonnet of a car, scowling even more deeply than usual.

There was no sign of the van, nor of Greg or his bike. Apart from that, the meadow was as Chris had last seen it.

'Who are this lot?' whispered Freckles to her partner.

Chris knew he could provide the answer, but said nothing. The police officers opened the gate and walked through with Chris trailing slowly behind them. For now they had forgotten the part he was supposed to play in their visit and were concentrating on the unexpected strangers.

Rat and a dark-haired woman stepped forward as the two coppers approached. The two groups came towards each other like gunfighters in an old Western.

'Hello,' the dark-haired copper called, offering a thin smile. Rat just nodded. 'We had no idea anyone was camping here,' the policeman added.

Rat shrugged. 'We had no idea we had to let anyone know,' he fired back. 'This is common land, isn't it?'

The coppers were slowing their pace. Rat stopped in front of them, kicking at the ground with his feet. The woman placed herself at his elbow. If they were trying to make a barricade, it didn't work. The dark-haired PC stopped to speak to them, but Freckles just walked round, aiming towards the vehicles. Rat turned his head, wincing as if he had toothache. He twitched back and forth, trying to see which of the two PCs he should intercept.

Chris watched all this with a growing sense of embarrassment. Each time the travellers looked away from the police, it was to glare at Chris. They were certain he had brought the police there to harass them.

'None of these vehicles is taxed,' WPC Freckles said.

Rat shrugged. 'Perhaps things got lost in the post,' he said. 'We move around a lot.' Freckles's expression didn't change.

'I don't suppose they're insured, either,' she commented. Rat said nothing, but just glowered at Chris. Everyone here knew that the vehicles were never going to be taxed, insured, MOTd or anything else which involved paperwork or sums of money over a tenner. The discussion was just a game. The police were showing that they had the power to make life difficult; the travellers were showing they didn't care.

'Excuse me . . .' Chris said, in a quiet voice.

The scar-faced PC turned back fractionally, not looking away from Rat but inclining his head so that he could hear what Chris was about to say.

'I thought we came here to look for Russell.'

He was hoping that the reminder might convince Rat that he hadn't brought the cops here to spy on his people. Failing that, he'd settle for getting on with the search and then leaving the meadow.

'In a moment, Chris,' the policeman replied.

'I have to go soon,' Chris insisted. 'I've got football practice.'

PC Scar wasn't that interested in what Chris had to do, but he and his partner had seen all they needed to. The travellers had broken so many rules, they could come back and play the tax disc game anytime. More likely, the travellers would move on, and the problem would be someone else's.

'OK,' he said, still facing away, 'why don't you lead us to where you saw your mate last.'

Rat seemed to get the message that the two coppers were going to play a different game for now, and stepped back. PC Scar walked past, but he didn't stop looking at the big, balding man until he was several paces beyond him, walking through the encampment.

Chris trailed behind.

'Strange company you keep,' whispered Rat as he went by. Chris didn't answer.

The only person in the camp left in sight was Kim, perched on the car, glaring hotly at the WPC. His teeth were bared in a warning grin, his eyes shining. For a moment, the mocking cruelty in that stare was almost familiar . . .

Chris walked on. The two police officers had paused and were waiting for him to direct them. He pointed across the common to the left. The three of them marched slowly over the meadow.

'You know those people?' asked Scar.

'Not really,' said Chris. He decided to come completely clean. 'We played football against them.'

'Strange friends for a boy like you,' Freckles commented. Chris decided she wouldn't want to hear that the travellers had made the same observation about them.

'Over here . . .' he said quietly, stepping over a patch of low, scrubby bushes on his way to the boundary ditch.

The ground was falling away very slightly already. By the time they came into the shade of the tree, Chris, looking back, saw that they were almost out of sight of the camp. It was almost as if Russell had been creeping along here to spy on the travellers. Why? What possible connection could he have with them?

'If your mate's mixed up with that lot, he could be in all kinds of trouble,' observed PC Scar.

'I'm not sure he is,' Chris replied, lamely.

'Wouldn't be a surprise to me,' Scar continued. 'The Jones boys have always been nothing but trouble.'

Freckles clambered down the side of the ditch, trying to hold on to her baton, her radio and her dignity with just two hands. Scar was obviously an equal opportunities sort of guy, because he let her slither down towards the bottom of the dry (fortunately) gully without moving a muscle to help.

'You've got it all wrong about Russell,' Chris protested, with a little more feeling this time. He heard the copper make a small snorting sound, which didn't sound like 'I'm sure you're right'. 'No, really, the only time he was ever close to any kind of trouble was when he was with his brother, Mick.'

Who kidnapped promising young strikers, said a voice in the back of his mind. Let's not forget that.

PC Scar turned to face Chris, and there was a very confident smile on his face. It made Chris feel very cold, as if . . .

Oh, oh.

'Well, there you are then,' Scar said after the briefest of pauses.

Chris waited to hear the next words, his heart hammering even though he knew what was coming. Perhaps *because* he knew what was coming.

'Didn't you know? Mick Jones is out.'

Thirteen

WPC Freckles was poking about in the dirt at the bottom of the ditch, turning over dead leaves with her shoe.

'Someone's been here, watching the camp,' she said. 'You can see where the grass is trampled.

'Anything else?' her partner asked.

'A few sweet wrappers and other junk,' she replied. 'Nothing recent. Our friend might have been here before today.'

'You might as well come out, then,' Scar said. He turned to walk back to the top of the slope, from where he would have a better view back towards the camp. It was only after that that he realised Freckles was struggling to get back up the bank, and reached out a hand to help.

'Watching the camp?' he said, thinking out loud. 'What would that be about, then?'

'I don't know,' muttered WPC Freckles, dusting herself off. She turned to Chris as if she expected answers.

But Chris had only questions. And they were tumbling around in his head like clothes in a washing machine. Sometimes one would stay at the front long enough to identify itself, but mostly it was just a confused jumble.

'Out?!' he choked. 'Mick Jones is out?'

'You weren't told?' asked Scar. He rubbed his chin. 'That's odd. He's been out for just over a month.'

'Out??' Chris spluttered again.

Since Mick Jones's arrest, Chris hadn't really had to think much about him. There had been interviews at the police station, forms to fill in, more interviews, that sort of thing, but after a month it all died down. There was such a rich storehouse of charges the police could bring against Jones – theft, arson, resisting arrest – they decided not to get too involved in Chris's abduction. After all, it wasn't a real kidnapping, they'd said. No ransoms or anything like that. And Mick Jones had insisted that he had never meant to harm Chris, just to keep him out of the way.

So when it was explained that Chris would have to go through a lot of fuss and bother if the abduction charge was brought, Chris and his father had agreed it should be dropped. Who needed court appearances? Mick was dead to rights on the arson and the theft charges anyway.

Since then, Mick had been remanded in prison awaiting trial. Chris was amazed at how long it took to bring a case to court, but it was no longer his concern. Besides, bringing up the subject would have put a lot of strain on his new friendship with Russell. The last he had heard, Chris had been told Mick Jones was due to appear in court after the New Year.

'How can he be out?' he demanded.

PC Scar was surprised by the strength of Chris's voice.

'Look . . .' he began.

'Just tell me what happened!' Chris insisted.

Scar was too off-balance to speak. His partner, now safely on the bank with them, started the explanation.

'He's been given bail. There have been a number of complications with the case and . . .'

'Complications?'

She bit her lip, gathered her wits, and tried again.

'Most of the theft charges have been dropped. The evidence wasn't as solid as we had hoped. And Mick's lawyer has been making a lot of accusations about police brutality at the time of the arrest, trying to provide a smokescreen for the resisting arrest charges . . .'

'They'd better not drop that charge,' her mate said, rubbing the bright red line along the angle of his jaw.

Freckles flicked a glance back at him, then turned back to Chris. 'The only really solid charge was the arson – you know, setting fire to the clubhouse at the university . . .'

'I know what arson is,' snapped Chris, irritably.

'Sure. Anyway, Mick has managed to persuade a psychiatrist that the fire was just a one-off, and that he isn't capable of doing anything like that again. So, he reapplied for bail and got it. He'll be on the outside until the trial.'

That was it? After all Mick Jones had done, all he had to say was that PC Scar had hit him first, and then produce a note from his doctor, and he was off the hook? Chris had more trouble dodging detention at school!

'He'll be back inside soon enough . . .' Scar said, strongly.

'Not soon enough for me,' Chris muttered.

WPC Freckles put her hand on Chris's shoulder. 'Don't worry,' she said. 'We don't have any report of him coming back this way. And he has no reason to come after you . . .'

'What?'

She stepped back. Chris's voice had come at her like a piece of hot fat from a frying pan, spitting with heat.

'There's no danger,' she continued, stumbling over the words.

Chris felt his temperature continue to rise. 'You think that's the problem? You think I'm afraid he'd come back and try to grab me again?' His voice was growing higher and louder. WPC Freckles was not a tall woman, but she had the advantage of being further up the slope. It must have been quite a shock to her to be bowled over by the rage pouring out of someone whose face was down below her belt buckle.

'I'm not frightened – I'm *furious*! Why didn't anyone tell me?' A thought flashed into his mind. 'Does Russell know?'

The police officers shrugged. Chris started to realise that they were the wrong targets for his fury, but since they were all he had, he didn't stop.

'Look, if the other charges were starting to look a bit thin, why didn't anyone think to go back to the abduction? They wouldn't have let him out then, would they?'

'It's a bit late to go back to that . . .' Freckles said. 'Besides, it was agreed you shouldn't be involved. It was thought it might be too hard for you to go into the witness box and –'

'Mick Jones doesn't frighten me!' Chris insisted. 'I face tougher guys than him in the penalty box – week in, week out.' The words had tumbled out before Chris had time to think. They were almost true. 'I can handle Mick; I'm not afraid of him. But can you handle him?'

The two police officers looked at him blankly. 'You say he's not in the area,' Chris continued. 'How do you know? Mick was always good at sneaking around, keeping out of sight. For all you know, he's slipped back to Oldcester; for all you know, he's somewhere near here right now. It wouldn't surprise me if he wasn't close enough to hear every word we're saying!!!'

That idea seemed to faze the coppers even more than Chris's lengthy outburst. Freckles looked around, peering into the nearby bushes. Scar rubbed his jaw again.

'Great . . .' muttered Chris, some way short of being filled with confidence.

A car engine in the middle distance made them all start. As one, they climbed to the top of the bank and looked back towards the camp. The battered old Renault Kim had been parked on was moving off towards the gate. Chris couldn't make out who was driving. He could see Rat and most of the other adults from the group; in fact, the only one he couldn't see (other than Greg, of course) was Kim.

'Great!' he said again, louder this time. 'Just great!!!'

'We'd better get you home,' said Freckles in a low voice, almost apologising.

Chris glanced at his watch. 'No thanks,' he said. 'I've got to get to London Road for training. You can give me a lift.'

Without waiting for an answer, Chris stalked off across the meadow. The two PCs looked at each other quickly. Freckles shrugged and they both set off in pursuit.

A full minute after they had departed, the branches of the tree rustled. A few small branches cracked as a dark shadow lowered itself to the ground. Swathed in a long, dark coat, the figure would have been hard to distinguish even if anyone had been looking back this way. But the tree-climber was careful not to be seen. It was something he was very good at.

As soon as he had dropped to the ground, he slid down the bank so that he was completely out of sight, then scuttled away towards the railway embankment, moving quickly and silently.

Fourteen

———— ⚽ ————

That afternoon, Chris worked harder in training than ever.

Even during the warm-up, he was on overdrive. They did some fast sprints back and forth across the pitch, and The Terminator, who often shouted himself hoarse hurrying the boys along, got left behind.

Then there was a complicated co-ordination exercise involving throwing a football round a circle; each player wore a numbered vest and the boys had to throw the ball the instant the coach called a number, aiming it to the right target. Chris whipped the ball out so fast he threatened to kill someone.

They took some shoot-outs; Chris slammed the ball past every keeper he faced. They played five-a-side; Chris didn't need the other four. There was a half-hour session when they worked on special tactics for the England games. It gave the boys a chance to draw breath and recharge their batteries. Chris, though, was on his feet throughout, asking questions, making suggestions. Sean Priest had threatened to sit on him if he didn't take a rest.

In the last game of the day, an eight-a-side match on the full pitch, Nicky was exhausted just watching Chris's work rate.

'Chris,' he gasped, leaning on his friend for support. 'England get here next weekend. This is just training, OK? It's just us.'

'Take the corner,' Chris snapped and he moved away so quickly Nicky almost collapsed to the ground.

It couldn't have been easier for Chris's team to score. Every time they won the ball, they looked up and there he was, in space, with a weary defender trailing in his wake. Although the coaches tried to encourage them to work on the skills and game plan they had talked about, it was always so much easier to hoof the ball to Chris and let him get on with it.

Watching from the sidelines, Sean Priest couldn't believe

what he was seeing. On the face of it, the only way to stop Chris was to ring the zoo and asked the guy who looked after the elephants to bring his dart gun.

'OK!' he called. 'Enough!! Hit the showers! Then I want ten minutes of your time to go over what we've learnt.'

Twenty-eight of the twenty-nine players selected to play in the two teams whooped with relief and ran off slowly towards the changing rooms, comparing notes and moaning good-naturedly about how tired they were. Priest looked around to decide which one of them he should call back to collect the practice balls. Chris was already doing it.

'Too much sugar . . .' Priest muttered and went off to talk to his fellow coaches.

Everyone was in a good mood after the session. It had gone well, and there were a few players (and a couple of the coaching staff) who were quietly confident they would give the England teams a good work-out. Priest was particularly pleased with the way some of the younger lads were shaping up. It wasn't that long since Oldcester had been regularly winning youth team competitions. Looking at some of the guys in the Under-11s and Under-12s, Priest was sure he could see another batch of medal-winning players.

Coming through a year or two above them, there were plenty of good individuals, not least Robbie James. Everyone had known James was an excellent defender when United signed him, but he had still managed to surprise everyone. His tackling was hard, but fair. He headed the ball well, and he was tall enough to win a lot of balls. Over the last few months, they had worked on his passing, and that was getting better. It was a pity he was so one-footed, but that was the only real fault in his game.

It was no surprise to Priest that England were taking a closer look at James. He was quality.

Having James in the squad made Priest proud, but he drew even more pleasure from the success of players the club had found and brought through. He was looking forward to the time when – a few seasons down the track – they pulled on first team shirts and ran out on to Star Park to play in the Premiership. Players like Chris Stephens and Nicky.

But more than any other player, Priest was looking forward to the day when Russell Jones won his place in the first team. The very fact that Jones had been so close to turning out wrong would make it even better if, one day, Priest could watch him turn out between the sticks for United. It was a day-dream Priest enjoyed more than most. And, right now, he knew it was going sour.

So, as soon as the coaches had debriefed the players, getting them to think about the good and bad points of the day's play, Priest called Chris and Nicky over. The most private place he could find for their conversation was the inside of his car. He needn't have bothered; everyone there knew what the three of them were talking about.

'Well?' he asked.

Chris still seemed full of fire, but it was Nicky who replied.

'We still haven't seen Russell,' he said in a quiet voice. 'We went out to his house this morning, but . . .'

Priest waited. He knew there was bad news coming, but he couldn't begin to guess what had gone wrong.

'But?'

'But there was no-one there except his sister. It's almost as if all the others have disappeared or something. The place is a complete tip – worse than usual.'

Priest nodded, even though Nicky's news hardly made the situation any clearer. 'Why do you think they've moved away?'

Nicky shot a quick look at Chris, hoping his team mate might take over. Chris sat perfectly still in the front seat, coiled like a spring, but not ready yet to say a word. Nicky decided to let Sean in on the rest of the good news.

'I don't think they have just moved away. I mean, Marie got left behind . . . oh, and there's one more thing . . . the police are looking for Russell.'

Priest jumped in his seat, almost breaking the steering wheel. 'What?!' he cried.

Nicky offered him a weak, sickly smile, and a brief report on what had happened that morning, up to the point where he had gone off in the ambulance with Marie. He sketched over the bit where she had told him Russell was the one who had frightened her. Nicky hated being in trouble so much he couldn't bear to be near anyone else in strife. Two hours sitting in casualty hadn't made him feel any more contented with life either. And he'd had to promise to go back later.

Priest turned back to the front. 'Chris?'

When Chris broke his silence, it was like a clap of thunder

from a storm that had crept up silently, and then thrown down a barrage of rain. The lightning in his eyes flashed.

'Did you know Mick Jones was out of prison?' he asked.

Priest had seen plenty of Nicky's temper over the last few years. It was short, sharp and over in seconds. This was different. Every muscle in Chris's face was clenched. His hands were balled tightly.

'What has that –?' Priest began. But he knew at once precisely what Mick Jones had to do with Russell's problems. It hadn't been that long since Mick had stolen some of Sean's souvenirs, stuff from when he was a player, stuff he could never have replaced if Chris and Nicky hadn't found it. Mick's shadow had fallen over all of them.

'You knew?' Chris snapped, not waiting for a reply.

Priest prided himself on treating the players at United like adults – even some of the twenty-year-olds. The same rule applied, from the youngest players up. It meant that, right now, no matter how hard he wanted to, Priest couldn't lie to Chris.

'Yes. The police told me last month.'

'Who else?'

Priest touched his tongue to his lip. 'Sorry?'

'Who else knew?'

Sean started to say that he couldn't be sure, that he hadn't actually been told anything like that. Then he looked at Chris's determined, angry expression and realised he was wrong. That he had been wrong keeping silent.

'Your school, I think. I guess your dad too. People who needed to keep their eyes open in case Mick came back.'

'But you didn't tell me. No-one told me.'

Priest waited a moment. 'No,' he answered.

'I see. And did Russell know?'

Once again, Priest thought carefully: 'I don't think so.'

For the first time in several minutes, Chris shifted in his seat. He stretched upright, and bit his lip hard.

'Look, Chris,' Priest continued. 'I told you before. I want you to concentrate on football. Every time some other attraction appears, you chase off after it. Sooner or later, it was bound to get you into trouble.'

'But I'm not the one in trouble, am I?'

Priest narrowed his eyes. 'What do you mean?'

Chris was staring out through the windscreen, looking off

across the car park. A few of the other guys were leaving the training ground, glancing at Sean's car as they left.

'Last time, when Mick was around, everyone made this big fuss about me getting kidnapped. But that wasn't the real problem. I mean, it wasn't about me. Mick was only ever interested in Russell. It's the same now. Mick's back, I know he is. And Russell's in trouble.'

They all took a moment to think. Nicky fidgeted uncomfortably in the back.

'He's right, Sean,' Fiorentini said at last. 'On the way to the hospital, Marie told me what happened to her. It was Russell who smashed the place up. It was Russell who locked her in the cupboard.'

It was almost more than any of them were ready for, but they had to face the truth. If this was what had really happened, there could be no place for Russell in England's plans, or United's. It really did look as if Russell Jones had turned bad once more.

And this time there could be no way back.

'Well I don't believe it!' Mac yelled. His face was flushed with emotion. Even though he was the smallest of the group, he seemed to have swelled up in size, so that Chris and the others had all been forced to take a step back.

'Steady on, Mac . . .' Jazz began.

Mac was anything but steady. 'What is this? How can you believe Russell would do stuff like that?'

No-one wanted to go over the evidence again. Mac looked around the group, from one face to another. The silence just made him even more annoyed.

'Don't you remember last time? You thought Russell was a crook then.'

There were a few mutters of agreement. It was Fuller, though, who spoke loudest: 'Yeah – and he was.'

Which was true, but not in the way that it sounded.

'Yeah, OK! But not because he wanted to be. Mick was making him steal. And he stopped!' Mac's small voice echoed around the playground. There was quite a crowd watching. Every time Mac looked round, they pretended they were doing something else, but the fact was that just about all of middle school was hanging on his every word.

'All he cares about is playing football!' Mac said, coming to the end of Russell's defence. 'He wouldn't get involved in anything bad again!'

The hundred or so kids on the 'jury' whispered to each other. There had been virtually no other topic of conversation at Spirebrook all day.

'So where is he?' asked Griff, one of the older boys who knew Russell well. Griff had been captain of the lower school football team when Russell came along. He was now playing in the upper school team, along with Chris and Nicky – and Russell. 'He's not in school today, right?'

Chris and Nicky shared a quick look. Every lesson, they had been aware of Russell's empty chair.

Their answer wasn't needed. There were plenty of others present who could agree. Everyone knew that no-one had seen Jones since Mac had lost sight of him on Saturday.

Chris knew different, of course, but he hadn't even told Nicky he had seen Russell creeping around Horton's Meadow. For one thing, he wasn't sure what that proved. It was suspicious, sure, but Chris didn't believe for a moment Russell had been planning to steal from Greg and his people – what would be the point?

At the same time, what possible reason could Russell have had for being there?

Chris turned his mind back towards the noisy discussion around him. Lunch was almost over. So far, he had barely eaten a thing.

'What was that warning to Chris to stay away?' Fuller was asking. Chris realised Nicky must have fed this part of the story to the group. There were never any secrets at Spirebrook.

'Maybe he's ill or something!' Mac insisted.

'He's sick all right,' muttered Fuller

Mac protested, with some help from Jazz and some of the others. Griff shouted him down.

'What about what his sister said? Tell them, Nicky . . .'

It was the single biggest piece of evidence they had that something had gone wrong. After practice, Nicky had phoned just about everyone in the football group to tell them what Marie had said – that Russell had been smashing up the house, and had frightened her into hiding in the cupboard.

Nicky looked uncomfortable and miserable, but he agreed that Griff's version of the story was more or less all of it. Marie had pointed the finger at Russell. And, from what he had picked up since, the police were looking for Russell in a big way, wanting to find out just what had happened to his parents and his young brother.

'Will you get real!' Mac raged. 'What are you saying? That Russell killed his whole family and dumped them in the river?'

It was a crazy idea, but in the absence of another theory which could shoot that one down, it was hard to trash it.

'Chris – for Pete's sake – will you tell them?!'

Chris looked up from the still-full bag that contained his lunch. Everyone was looking at him, waiting for him to supply the answer. After all, he'd been there with Nicky when Marie was found; he was the one who led the police to look for Russell. Plus, he was Chris. He always had the answers.

'I don't know . . .' he whispered.

Mac threw his hands up in despair and turned away. Several others muttered to each other, as if Chris had just given them the facts clearly. The tide of opinion was turning very sharply against Russell Jones.

'So what about these people on Horton's Meadow?' asked one of the girls at the edge of the group. 'Couldn't they be involved?'

'How?' asked Griff, who had appointed himself head of the prosecution, a role Nicky normally filled. 'They're just gypsies.'

'Actually, they aren't proper gypsies,' Jazz corrected him.

Griff let that slide by. 'Whatever. They don't matter.'

'Yeah, but the police don't like them . . .' Steve 'Bruise' Brewster called from the middle of a small group of guys who had decided to stick up for Russell.

'The Old Bill don't like anyone,' Griff commented.

'But what are they doing on the meadow?' asked Doughnut. 'And why did that Greg bloke disappear so fast when the police arrived at Russell's place?'

'And what's this about Mick Jones being back?' said Lucas, who received a sharp nudge in the ribs from Mac, who gestured towards Chris with his eyes as a reminder.

Chris knew the guys – along with everyone else, it seemed – were worried to say Mick's name in case he freaked out. He felt a last surge of the anger he had shown with Sean Priest, but bit his lip and said nothing. He and his father had already had a pretty solid row about it, and Chris had made sure Mrs Cole knew how he felt too. There had been times over the last couple of days when Chris wondered if he shouldn't have words with the guy in the newsagents – everyone seemed to know Mick was out before he did.

Nicky was looking over Chris's shoulder, peering into the paper bag containing his lunch. Chris glanced back, then held the bag towards his friend. It took him a moment to realise that Nicky wasn't scrounging for food, but was wondering why Chris wasn't eating. Of course, once it was offered, Nicky dipped in and took a sandwich.

'Too many questions,' Nicky said before he filled his mouth with the food. His face twisted with distaste when he realised that it was only plain cheese and that the bread wasn't fresh.

'That's for sure,' Chris said, 'and not enough answers.'

Nicky nodded, chewing quickly and swallowing. 'You OK?' he mumbled through the last pieces of food.

Chris turned round. Did Nicky think he was frightened of Mick Jones as well? Didn't anyone understand?

'Yeah,' he said, coolly. 'I just used up all my energy yesterday.'

Nicky grinned, flashing his white teeth. He sat back again, brushing back his long fringe. 'You were wild!' he giggled.

Chris grinned back. 'This business with Russell is bugging me,' he explained. 'I hate not being able to do anything.'

Nicky's smile faded. He looked around to see who else was listening and realised they were the centre of a small bubble, with conversations all around them, but a small, quiet zone in the middle. It was like the centre of a hurricane.

'Who says we can't do anything?' Nicky asked.

Chris looked into his mate's eyes and knew Nicky wasn't mucking around. It was the Fiorentini way – there wasn't a problem you couldn't just run straight through. Whereas Chris was full of concerns about what other people had told him – his father, Mrs Cole, Sean Priest, the police – Nicky only cared about what Chris thought.

So Chris thought about what they knew, and what they had seen. He thought about Mick Jones, Greg and the travellers, and Russell. In the back of his mind, there was an image of the game taking place next weekend without Russell.

'No-one . . .' said Chris.

Fifteen

Deciding that they were going to deal with the Russell Jones situation was one thing, finding time to do something was another.

Monday, school and homework; Tuesday, school and school soccer practice; Wednesday, school and after-school match. Chris and Nicky filed out of the dressing room last and next to last, urging their team mates into action even before the kick-off. They had plans for the evening that didn't include extra time or penalties . . .

It was a County Schools Cup match against Eastbury, a tough first round draw. This wasn't the first time Chris and Nicky had played them. In their very first season playing for the 'Brook, Eastbury had taken them 2–0. Chris remembered the game vividly – he had been marked so tightly he only really touched the ball three times – once at each kick-off.

Hassan Black, a team mate of Chris and Nicky's at United, also played for Eastbury. He had been winding up his team mates for weeks about how Spirebrook thought they were hot now they had four players in the United youth team.

'Hey, Blackie!' yelled Nicky across the pitch as the two teams prepared for the game. 'Did you tell 'em which four of us it is?'

Hassan grinned back. 'Don't worry, Nicky, we know who we have to take care of.'

Eastbury were in a new all-white strip; Spirebrook were in red and blue. From the beginning, the marking was so tight that from a distance it must have looked like ten Union flags were being waved on the pitch.

Nicky had a tussle with a long-limbed guy with razor-cut hair playing at left back; Jazz found himself face to face with Hassan; Bruise lived up to his reputation by mistiming a tackle on Eastbury's lone striker – both were limping from that moment on. Hassan bent the free kick against the bar with the goalie beaten.

As they waited for the goal kick, Hassan trotted past Chris.

'Hey, Stephens – where's Russell?'

'We don't know.'

'He still hasn't turned up?' Hassan asked, amazed at the news. 'Does Sean know? What's happening about next Sunday?'

'I don't know,' said Chris, sharply. This wasn't a discussion he wanted to have.

Hassan watched Mac line up to take the goal kick. For a moment he looked quite worried (for Russell?), then his face took on a new look of confidence. 'Come on, Eastbury!' he called. 'Let's keep the pressure on them at the back.'

Mac looked daggers at him. Hassan might as well have yelled 'hit lots of shots at the short goalkeeper'.

Chris also gave Hassan a hot look. The midfielder at least had the decency to offer an apologetic shrug. Come the weekend, they'd be in the same team together, facing England. In the meantime, it was Spirebrook vs Eastbury in the County Cup. Nothing else mattered.

Chris cleared his head of all the thoughts that were cluttering it up and urged his team mates to work harder. The Union flags waved a little faster.

Chris's marker was a player he knew well. The guy was a solid, powerful lad with short black hair and a hard, square chin that suggested he would have taken up karate instead of football if the kit had been better. In that previous game, he had been Chris's marker. More recently, he had been in the Eastbury Town youth team that had played the Riverside Colts last year. Chris had managed to turn the tables on him that time, scoring twice as the Colts ran off 4–1 winners.

It looked as if the guy was determined to get things back to the old ways this time. He clattered Chris with a late tackle in the tenth minute; and five minutes later barged him down as they both jumped for a header.

After the second challenge, Chris picked himself off the floor slowly. It felt like his opponent had put on quite a bit of size since the last game. It felt like getting thumped by a train.

The ref spoke to the defender, but Chris knew that from then on his opponent would behave himself anyway. Those early challenges had been designed to rough Chris up a little, to get him worried. The defender was a big lad, and he was explaining to Chris that he could expect that kind of treatment all afternoon.

Chris dropped back for a few moments to catch his breath, leaving Phil Lucas alone up front. He caught the black-haired defender looking at him, grinning with satisfaction.

'Right . . .' muttered Chris to himself.

The game stayed very tight — there was little room to move. Slowly, though, as the least fit players tired, things began to loosen up. Nicky found that his lanky opponent was quick, but had little stamina. Nicky tested him with a few runs off the ball and found the boy being left further and further behind.

Half-time was getting close when Nicky tested the boy again, this time with the ball at his feet. He half beat him on the outside, then cut back again as the full back chased him down. He was almost up to the front corner of the penalty box before the defender got some help.

At once, Nicky looked up. Chris was tracking across the box, arm raised, moving steadily. The black-haired defender was right at his elbow.

'Yes, come on!!!' called Chris, and Nicky instinctively laid the ball forward off the inside of his right boot, playing it very slightly to Chris's right to keep it further away from the defender.

The black-haired Eastbury player saw the pass almost as quickly as Chris, and tried to close him down. Having been on the receiving end of a couple of clattering tackles already, surely Chris wouldn't fancy another one. The defender stayed close, but held off the challenge. He didn't want to give away a free kick to a tackle from behind.

Chris could feel the other player at his heels, and slowed fractionally so that his opponent was almost touching him. The ball slid across the turf towards his right foot. Nicky was moving into what space he could find; Chris could just knock the ball back with his right peg. Or he could lay the ball off with his left.

The option he chose was much riskier. As the ball bobbled in front of him, Chris scooped it up with the toe of his right boot, flicking it round behind him. In the same instant, he rolled around to his right, actually bouncing off the defender.

Black Hair was too close to use his feet, too slow to use his body. Chris felt his opponent's hands reaching out to grab him, but by then it was too late.

Chris shoved himself clear. His spinning turn had brought him behind the defender and into space. The Eastbury keeper's eyes opened in alarm. It must have seemed as if Chris had teleported in from nowhere.

Before anyone could gather their wits, Chris let fly with his left foot. Naturally two-footed, Chris had always been able to shift his balance in a split-second. On this occasion, he'd touched the ball on with his right, taken two short steps and then fired off his left, all in a few fractions of a second. The keeper hadn't even thought about which way to dive when the ball whistled past him to his right, low and hard. A defender arriving at the back post got a touch, but that only helped the ball into the net.

The rapid turn he had made finally caused Chris to slip a little, but the goal was his and he didn't mind hitting the floor for his pains. He heard Nicky and Phil Lucas roaring 'Yes!!!' nearby, and the couple of dozen spectators breaking into a cheer a moment later.

Better still, he heard the defender utter a sharp swear word. He'd been reeled in like a fish on a hook.

'I don't believe you!' the black-haired lad sighed, shaking his head. Chris was being hauled to his feet by Nicky. They banged heads to celebrate, then both of them were knocked back to the ground again as Phil Lucas and Jazz arrived. Laughing in celebration, the 'Brookers struggled to their feet once more, and turned to head back to their own half.

Nothing changed in the match by half-time, 'That was a sweet goal,' was the only comment Flea offered, but it was clear he was pleased. It was still a close game, but Eastbury were being forced into opening up now they were 1–0 down. There was a good chance Spirebrook could get another couple early in the second half and settle the tie.

'That would leave us a couple of hours to get out to Horton's Meadow,' Nicky whispered to Chris. Chris nodded without looking across at his team mate. He took a long drink from a bottle of a sweet, banana-flavoured drink Flea had produced. The boys hadn't been sure about it at first. When Flea told them it had been made by a domestic science class, they were even less convinced. In fact, it tasted OK. Of course, this didn't mean that he wanted to know what was in it, or who might have had a hand in making it.

'What are you two whispering about?' demanded Mac grumpily. He was pulling at the collar of the goalkeeper's jersey as if it was choking him. Chris had already noticed that it looked a bit small.

'Nothing!' said Nicky, quickly. It didn't convince Mac at all.

'You're up to something, aren't you?' Mac demanded. 'I heard you talk about Horton's Meadow.' Each 'r' rolled slightly as Mac spoke it. He hadn't been in Scotland for a long time, but his accent always seemed to come back when he was angry. Nicky, who could manage to sound as if he was from Sicily, east London or darkest Peru depending on his mood, believed it was because it was easier to threaten someone in a Scottish accent.

Nicky pouted, annoyed that the secret had been penetrated so easily. 'Why don't you speak up a bit?' he hissed. 'I don't think they quite heard you on the other side of the pitch.'

'Is this something to do with Russell?'

Chris hesitated, wondering if he could get away with pretending that he and Nicky were still on the trail of the site of the Equinox Fair. Unfortunately, Nicky was already spilling the beans by then.

'Yes! We're going to try and get out there and poke around; find out what Greg and his mates are up to.'

Mac shuffled across so that he was a little closer. 'You think they're . . . I don't know . . . nicking stuff, or something?' Mac's imagination was a bit limited when it came to criminal activity.

'How else do you think they make a living?' Nicky asked.

'And you think they've got Russell involved?'

'What do you think?' Nicky asked with one of his big shrugs thrown in for good measure.

Mac thought about this for a moment, his eyes gazing off into the distance as if he was trying to see something through a dark, dirty mist. He shuffled away. Chris noticed him exchange a few quick words with Jazz.

'Why did you tell him that?' Chris asked Nicky. 'You don't really think that's what's happening, do you?'

Nicky was grinning broadly, as if he was really pleased with himself. 'Hey, it got rid of him, didn't it?' he boasted.

Mac shuffled closer once again.

'OK, me and Jazz are coming too,' he said, with a 'and you can't stop us' note in his voice. Chris made a face at Nicky.

'Mac, the more of us there are crashing around, the easier it will be for Russell to see us.'

Mac listened seriously, but it was clear he wasn't going to be put off. 'You and Nicky have convinced yourselves Russell's gone bad again. I don't believe that. Russell's going to need his friends there if –'

Something about the way Mac put it annoyed Chris. He jumped in quickly before Mac said any more.

'Hang on! What makes you so certain we're not Russell's mates any more?'

'Are you?' said Mac, and he wasn't very friendly about it.

Chris leant a little closer so that he could get his point across forcefully without being overheard. 'Let's get one thing straight, Mac. I'm trying to help Russell. This England thing is the biggest chance any of us have ever had, and Russell is blowing it. I can't stop Sean from giving Russell's place to Gillespie if Russell doesn't turn up for training. He's the one acting weird, remember – not us.'

The air of certainty around Mac faded a little. 'So, you're not saying Russell's become a crook again?'

'No! Why would I?'

Mac's mouth twisted in a sorry little grimace. 'I thought you and Nicky might be, you know, a little jealous?'

'Jealous?!' Nicky howled angrily. If there was anyone around them who hadn't been tuned into their conversation before, they were now. Chris tried to calm his team mate down. He didn't succeed.

'You little berk, Mac!' Nicky barked loudly. 'What, you think we're jealous of this business of the England people taking a look at Jones and Robbie flamin' James? Get real! We're better players than either of them!'

Chris winced, partly because Nicky was shouting loud enough to make sure everyone knew exactly how he felt, and partly because he had managed to make it sound like Chris felt the same. Over in the distance, Robert 'flaming' James was sitting with the lower school team, in a state of shock. Chris looked away, trying again to shut Nicky up somehow.

'What Nicky is trying to say . . .' he started, but he couldn't complete the sentence. Nicky had said *exactly* what he wanted to say.

Mac was back in an argumentative mood once again. 'Yeah, well, we'll see, won't we? In the meantime, Jazz and I are coming with you.'

'Fine!' snapped Nicky. 'So just concentrate on making sure you keep a clean sheet, then. We can't afford to let this game go into extra time.'

'Fine!' Mac retorted. The silence that fell on the group once the two of them had stopped shouting was like a thunderclap. Everyone looked down at the ground, or stared at the label on their drinks bottle, trying hard not to catch anyone else's eye. A few moments later, Flea walked over and suggested that maybe they'd like to start the second half. Chris looked round. Eastbury were already on the pitch.

There was one less spectator at the end of the game than at the beginning. By the time he slipped away from his hiding place over by the tennis courts, Russell had already seen that Spirebrook didn't have to worry about extra time. They were losing 3–1.

'What does it take to get you guys to back off?' Russell sighed. He honestly didn't know the answer.

Sixteen

'Well, we've found out one thing at least,' said Jazz, with the slightest of smiles.

Mac looked at him with an expression of pure venom in place. 'And what's that?' he said, crisply.

'We know where the Equinox Fair is going to take place.'

Mac opened his mouth to explain to Jazz just how important that information wasn't any more, but he managed to hold back the words. Instead, he followed Jazz's gaze across the corner of the meadow, to where there was a tall hedge. Beyond it, he knew, there was a large, rising field. From where they were lying, at the edge of the ditch Chris had led the police officers to before, the two boys could see the coloured awnings of sideshow tents, part-built structures on which the bigger rides would be fixed, and a huge flag-pole.

Mac pulled his jacket closer. The evening was already pretty cool, and there were dark clouds in the sky threatening rain. He didn't like the idea of getting soaked as part of Chris and Nicky's master plan.

'I guess it isn't going to be a secret for very much longer, is it?' he said.

Jazz agreed, smiling. The smile faded slowly over the next few seconds as Jazz considered what he had just heard. He looked across the meadow towards the field again, listening to the sounds of men working hard to get everything ready for the weekend.

'You knew they were going to use those fields?' he asked at last.

Mac nodded. 'My dad told me after I asked him what he was doing on the meadow.' He could see at once from Jazz's face that his team mate didn't understand. 'I couldn't tell Nicky that I knew, he'd have gone on *forever* about how clever he was figuring it out.'

'But those fields aren't actually part of Horton's Meadow, are they?' Jazz asked, although he really knew the answer already.

'Yeah, right,' scoffed Mac, 'you try telling Nicky that.'

Jazz smiled to show he agreed. A last point occurred to him. 'How come your father was actually on the meadow, though,' he asked, 'if the fair is going to be held on those fields?'

'They were thinking of using the meadow for car parking,' Mac explained. 'You can get to those fields OK from the main road, but there's not much room for the fair and all the car parking they need. So the council wanted to see if there was any way they could use this end of the common. They decided not to – everyone knows what it gets like when it rains.'

Mac looked up again at the darkness gathering overhead. To the north, there was so much dark cloud it looked as if a mountain range had grown up in the last few hours.

His eyes were then drawn along the horizon, following the line of the railway embankment as it curved around on the far side. He concentrated on the space between two tall trees. Jazz saw which way he was looking. They both concentrated hard, trying to pick out the signal they were waiting for against the dark sky. In the fading light, both wondered if maybe there wasn't a small plume of rising blue smoke.

'You think this plan is going to work?' Jazz asked after they had watched for a while longer.

Mac smiled. 'It's Chris and Nicky's plan,' he said. 'You know how carefully they think these things through.'

Jazz nodded, his lips set in a tight line. 'Yeah,' he said after a moment of remembering past adventures, 'but will it *work?*'

'Of course not,' muttered Mac.

They weren't the only ones to have noticed. Some distance away from their hiding place, a couple of the kids in the camp saw the column of smoke and pointed it out to each other. In the centre of the group, one face in particular watched the way the pale line spread out as it climbed and was scattered by the rising wind. Sapphire blue eyes glittered as they followed the rising plume of smoke. Finally, Kim turned towards the battered old Escort parked near the gate.

Nothing stirred. Kim took one last glance at the distant smoke, then turned away from the other kids and slid off towards the gate.

Meanwhile, not that far away, a figure in a long, dark coat was watching the same sign with a grim, tired look on his face. He passed a hand through his close, rust-coloured hair, and wondered what to do. He looked up at the nearby embankment – someone was up there, he saw, moving along the old railway like a ghost. Drawing his coat closer, the figure shrunk back into the shadows.

The two people with the best view of all, though, were Chris and Nicky. That was because they were right at the source of it.

Nicky coughed a couple of times after the wind caught the smoke and blew it around the yard. He made a face at Chris, who was standing across on the other side of the yard, near the house.

'This had better work . . .' he yelled.

'Shut up!' urged Chris, surveying their handiwork. 'What's the point of doing this if you're just going to let him know we're here.'

Nicky muttered something, then moved towards the small out-building at the end of the cottage. He stepped inside and pulled the door closed. 'Man, it stinks in here,' he called, but Chris didn't answer. Nicky looked out through a hole in the door. His partner had disappeared, probably into the house. 'Trust Chris to pick the best hiding place,' he moaned, and then settled back to wait.

Inside the house, Chris breathed a sigh of relief when Nicky finally shut up. He positioned himself in one of the upstairs rooms – Russell's, by the look of the decoration (the 'wallpaper' was made from cut-up football magazines). From the narrow window, he had a fair view of the yard outside.

Right in the centre, the rusting old oil drum continued to belch smoke. Chris had topped up the rubbish inside with some green wood and old rags which he knew would throw up a good cloud.

'Now all we need is for Russell to take the bait,' he said to himself. He had no doubt his mate would come to investigate the fire. He didn't even expect it would take long. In fact, the way the sky was clouding over, if Russell didn't see the smoke in the first twenty minutes, he'd be lucky to see it at all. The sun had long since disappeared and the evening was drawing in quickly. Chris wondered if they'd all get drenched before the night was through.

Meanwhile, though, he forced himself to concentrate. It was hard to make out much in the yard as the night closed in. The weak fire in the drum crackled and threw off more fumes than an old steam loco, but it didn't shed a lot of light. The area around the edge of the yard was in almost complete shadow.

He tried listening, but he couldn't do any better with that. The fire provided all the cracks and snaps he could handle – the idea that he'd hear someone sneaking up was a joke. Maybe this idea wasn't going to work out after all. Maybe, he thought, it was time to give up and go ho–

There. Was that something moving around the edge of the yard? Chris froze, his face pressed against the window. The shape had vanished, but he was sure he had seen someone over by the out-house. There was a chance it was Nicky, of course, giving up even more quickly than Chris, but he didn't think so. Whoever it was looked bigger, taller.

Chris took a moment to feel good about the way things were going, then stepped back from the window. He was just about to creep across the room and back towards the stairs when he heard a familiar voice cry out.

'Hey! Who's locked the door? Hey!! Chris!!!!'

Nicky. And he didn't sound happy.

'Damn!' Chris cursed under his breath. He thought about going back to the window to take a look, but decided against it. Moving as quietly but swiftly as he could, he crept on to the landing outside Russell's bedroom. There was no point being too subtle any more. They had been rumbled.

Reaching the top of the stairs, Chris looked down. The hall was dark, but he was pretty sure no-one was down there. All the same, there was a sudden tightness in his throat and a turning, rumbling feeling in his gut. He could hear Nicky calling from outside, but the voice sounded a long way away and Chris was suddenly aware of just how isolated they were.

As he took his first step down the stairs, there was a new noise. Someone was pushing at the front door. There was still a lot of junk piled up in the hall – after all, no-one had been here to tidy up – and the door opened only fractionally before it got caught up on some boxes and other rubbish.

Chris could see a hand on the edge of the door, pushing hard. He froze for a moment, watching it carefully. He wasn't frightened – in fact, he was stone-cold calm. All the same, he wanted to see how things turned out before he made another move.

The door shook with the force of the effort being used against it but it wasn't opening any wider. Chris decided that perhaps this meant whoever was on the other side couldn't hope to get through that way for another moment or two. That meant this might be a good time to be getting out through the back.

He took the remaining stairs steadily but quickly, his eyes glued to the front door. It was thrashing back and forward even more violently, and he thought he caught the sound of a voice growling with frustration. Still he felt no fear. After all, this was a good sign. The longer he could be sure that the intruder was at the front, the better that made his chances of getting out the back.

By the time he set foot down in the hall, Chris was feeling pretty confident. He was a little worried about how easy it might be to let Nicky out of the out-house, and then for the pair of them to make good their escape, but he was safe for the moment.

He turned away from the front door to make his way to the kitchen, checking the floor for any obstacles. That was when something fastened on his collar and yanked him back. And if the hall had been gloomy, that was nothing compared to the darkness that followed.

Seventeen

It was a very firm grip. One arm had locked about his neck, pulling his head back. Another hand was gripping his right wrist, wrenching his arm back painfully behind his back. It wasn't that Chris couldn't move, but he knew he would really understand what pain meant if he tried.

His attacker said just four words. 'Don't move; keep quiet.' The voice was a very hoarse, low whisper, spat into his ear from close by. He tried to work out if it was familiar, but decided that one threatening whisper sounded pretty much like all the rest. He also decided not to argue.

Instead, he tried to work out just what could be happening. After a moment of panic, he decided that there was no way he had been grabbed by whoever it was who had been battering at the front door. That was reassuring. Of course, whoever it was, they weren't exactly proving too friendly either, so perhaps he was being a little over-confident.

His mind raced as he tried to understand what was going on. The blackness which engulfed him was simple to understand. He was in the closet at the foot of the stairs, the same one in which they had found Marie. Whoever was currently holding him had been hiding in there and had seen Chris come down the stairs through a crack in the door or something. And that person didn't want to be discovered by whoever was at the door either.

Chris tried to take a deep breath (which wasn't easy with the pressure on his windpipe). Yeah, this wasn't so bad. So long as the person outside the house was a bad guy, the person behind him was probably OK. Perhaps. Of course, if the door batterer was trying to get in to rescue Chris, that meant . . .

The more he thought about it, the less Chris liked the

situation he was in. There was still a loud racket going on outside, so he decided to risk a question.

'Russell?' he croaked.

The arm around his neck tightened, pulling his chin back.

'Shut up!' the voice said again, which wasn't much of an answer. This time it sounded more familiar. Chris still couldn't decide if this was good news.

At that moment, the fierce rattling outside the front door ended. There was a grunted swear word, and then the sound of footsteps. Whoever it was – mad killer or the US Cavalry – they were moving away.

'He's gone ...' choked Chris, in case his attacker hadn't realised. To his relief, the grip around his throat relaxed a little.

'Don't be too sure. He's bound to try the back door ...'

Well, sure, thought Chris, I knew that. However, the pause gave them a few moments to talk.

'It is you, Russell, right?'

'Who did you think? Now shut up, Chris!'

Chris made a mental note never to offer to wrestle with Russell Jones again, and relaxed a little more. He was still being held quite firmly, but he knew that he was in no immediate danger. In fact, he gained the strong idea that he was being held like this for his own protection.

'Is that Mick outside?' he whispered, as quietly as he could.

'Will you keep quiet? I'm trying to listen!!!'

Chris did as he was told. If he could, he would have tried to make his heart beat a little more quietly. In the darkness, it seemed to be the only thing he could hear.

He recalled how noisy the floorboards in the hall were. He was sure they'd hear if anyone came in. All the same, he expected the closet door to be wrenched open any moment. Time passed very slowly.

'I thought I told you to keep out of this!' Russell hissed. The sudden voice made Chris jump, which was when he realised that both his hands were free again.

'I got your message,' he whispered. There was no reply from behind him. Chris concentrated on listening again. It occurred to him a moment later that he couldn't hear Nicky any more.

'We have to get out of here,' he said.

'Not yet,' came the voice from behind.

There was another silent wait in the dark. Chris could feel

111

his heart pounding. Thanks to Mick Jones, being locked in an enclosed space was a habit he would never enjoy.

Finally, he felt Russell moving past him, and there was a slow, steady creak as the door opened. There still wasn't a lot of light in the hall, but compared to the pitch black of the closet, it was quite bright. All the same, Chris took his time following Russell and only ventured into the hall when his team mate was close to the kitchen door.

'What's going on?' he asked, although the end of the sentence became the faintest whisper after Russell held up his hand for silence.

'He could still be outside,' Russell explained, almost mouthing the words rather than speaking them. Chris bit his lip. He was in no hurry to confront Mick again. At the same time, he realised that maybe this wasn't such good news for Nicky.

Russell had stepped into the kitchen. Chris stood in the doorway, eyes fixed past his friend to the back door, which hung crookedly from the bent and battered frame. The yard was dark and silent.

Russell crept silently across the floor. Two or three paces from the door, he halted, making a kind of clicking noise with his tongue. At once there came an answering click.

'OK?' Russell asked.

Chris was on the point of saying that, yeah, he was fine, but that he was worried about Nicky when another voice broke in. It was low and faint, but somehow familiar. Chris strained to hear what it said.

'Yeah, all clear. He's gone.'

'Good,' said Russell, flicking a fast look back at Chris. There was a weak smile on his face. 'OK, Chris, you can go now,' he added.

Chris didn't move. It seemed to him that moving out of the kitchen now would be a big mistake.

'Wait a minute, Russell,' he hissed. 'I didn't come all this way just to go back again without some answers.'

Russell wasn't interested in providing any. 'Look, we may not have much time — he could come back any minute.'

The voice in the yard whispered something urgently, although it was still so quiet Chris couldn't make out the words. He found himself taking a step forward just on the off-chance he would be able to hear, but he couldn't. Russell made a small gesture with his eyes, nodded his head and replied 'yes' to a question Chris wished he'd shared. Then he looked back at his friend once more.

'You have to get out of here! I can handle this.'

'Handle what, Russell?'

The muscles around his friend's eyes tightened as if he was in pain. Chris could feel how much of a hurry Russell was in to see him leave.

'It's my business, Chris! I know what I'm doing.'

'Is that right?' Chris fired back, allowing the volume of his voice to creep up a little too. 'Do you know what you're going to lose if you keep this up?'

A look of confusion passed across Russell's face. He looked more desperate than ever. Once again, there was a whisper from outside, and this time Chris caught something about someone being on the far side of the house, searching for something in that part of the yard that lay right under the embankment. Russell was biting his tongue hard, and screwing his eyes tight closed as he tried to get his thoughts in order.

When he opened them again, he stared right at Chris with fierce determination. Chris realised he had won a little time to explain.

'On Sunday, we're playing the England Schools Under-15s. It's something Sean has worked out, a sort of training match for both squads. Next spring, to celebrate the opening of the new school, we'll play the England Under-16s. Only, by then, you could be playing on the other side.'

He watched Russell's face as his friend registered what Chris was saying. 'That's right!' he added swiftly. 'The England people are thinking of inviting you and Robbie James to join a training camp at Lilleshall in a few weeks' time; their coach will be there on Sunday to take a look. So you figure it out; what are they going to think if you don't show?'

Russell was staring at the floor. Chris was sure he could hear his team mate grinding his teeth. Certainly he didn't look as thrilled with the news as he could have done.

'This only makes things worse . . .' he said, and there was a catch in his voice as if he was going to scream.

Chris had no idea how this news could be considered 'worse' (worse than what – being made King?); what was more, he knew he wasn't going to have it explained. All he could do was make sure Russell understood what was at stake. He owed his mate that much.

'Look, Russ, let's go explain things to Sean. I bet he'd –'

Russell looked up abruptly, fire in his eyes and a dark growl in his voice. 'No!' he insisted. 'You have to leave me alone!'

'Yeah, yeah,' Chris replied, making a cutting move with his hand to show that he wasn't listening. 'I got your warning before.'

'What?'

'You know; the message you gave Dr Loenikov . . .'

Russell's face remained blank. Chris took a moment to consider.

'That wasn't you?'

'You see?' Russell pleaded. 'If you don't back off, you'll only get dragged in deeper. Whatever he told you, whatever he told Dr Whatisface, he meant it. Stay away from this one, Chris, I can handle it.'

Russell moved into the doorway, glancing out into the yard. Did that mean his mysterious companion was gone? Chris listened carefully to see if anything was said, but all he could hear was some distant clattering, as if someone was throwing lumps of wood and old cans around, or playing the drums very badly.

'Oh, really?' Chris said. 'Like you've handled this? I mean, I knew that phoney fire scam would flush you out. If I can do it, so can he . . .'

'Shut up!!' Russell cried, letting his voice rise as much as he dared, it seemed. 'You just don't get it, do you?'

Chris knew he was making no headway. Perhaps this was a waste of time. Even so, he felt he had no choice but to make a final effort.

'Shall I tell you what I know, Russell? I know Mick's back. I know he's putting pressure on you like he used to. I know he's *using* you.' Chris stared hard at Russell, seeing what impact his words might be having. 'What I don't know is how much success he's having . . .'

Russell uttered a short, dry laugh. 'I heard you talking to those cops, Chris . . . I know what you think of me.'

Damn. That wasn't entirely unexpected, but it couldn't help if Russell knew Chris had developed a few doubts. He thought about trying to explain, but Russell looked on the point of

114

racing out through the door and he knew he didn't have much time.

'You've been acting real weird, Russ. People are worried about you. They see what's happened here – the way the house has been turned over, what happened to Marie, the way the rest of your family have split . . .'

He paused to let Russell consider what he had just said, then added: 'You can't handle Mick on your own, Russell,' he said quietly. 'You've got to let us help.'

Russell turned to face Chris again. The fading twilight outside lit one side of his face, while the other was hidden by the gathering evening gloom inside the kitchen. It made it very hard to read the expression in his eyes, but Chris could tell from the way Russell's voice hardened that he had hit a nerve.

'You're so wrong about this, Chris . . .'

Chris waited for Russell to explain in what way he was wrong, but there was a sudden heavy crash outside, and the sound of a distant, angry voice. Russell ducked down a little in the doorway, alarmed. He whipped his head back to hiss a command to Chris:

'You've got to get out of here, now!'

'Not until . . .' Chris began, still prepared to argue.

'Let me put it another way, Chris – I'm leaving. I don't think you want to be here on your own. Just take the lane and the short cut across the fields back to the main road.'

And with that, he disappeared.

Russell moved so fast Chris barely had time to blink, never mind do anything to stop his pal. By the time he'd recovered his wits and made it to the back door himself, there was no sign of Russell outside. He could hear some more angry words in the distance, but that was all.

Chris left the house at a low, skidding run, skipping across the yard and down the narrow lane that connected the cottage to the outside world. He didn't look back before he reached the first stile.

Nicky was waiting on the other side, crouched down under the hedge. He looked pale in the darkness. In fact, when his face appeared out of the shadows, it almost gave Chris a heart attack.

'What happened to you?' Chris asked urgently.

'How should I know?' Nicky replied, which wasn't a very useful answer. 'One moment I was hiding in the out-house like we agreed; then someone came along and locked the bolt on the outside of the door; then, ten minutes later, someone *unlocked* the door again and told me to get out of there.'

'Who was it?' Chris demanded. 'Did you recognise the voice?'

'No!!! Man, it freaked me out being caught like that! The second time, I looked over the top of the door, but I couldn't see anyone! Then I heard all this banging and stuff from the front of the house, like someone was tearing up the place all over again. Then there was more stuff out the back. Who —?'

'Mick. Who else? Just like we thought, the trick with the fire flushed him out just the same as it brought Russell back. Neither of them could just let their house get burnt down, could they? The only problem was that Mick must have some hidden way of getting here . . . unless . . .'

Nicky waited silently for Chris to finish, knowing that his strike partner was thinking through what had happened. Chris had fixed his mouth in a firm, straight line and his eyes were locked right ahead as he replayed the events of the last few minutes in his mind.

'Never mind. The fact is, we still have one surprise left that even Mick can't have expected. Hand me the radio.'

Nicky dipped into his pocket and pulled out a slim box which he handed to Chris. There was a small aerial on the top which extended as Chris telescoped it out. Thumbing a small switch on the side, Chris activated the walkie-talkie and pressed the talk button.

'Mac, are you there?'

'Yeah, I'm here! Are you —?'

Mac's voice was loud and clear over the speaker. The walkie-talkies were a present from his father, good quality models with a range of a couple of kilometres. Chris lost the end of the first message through turning down the volume too low.

'Never mind that now. Did you see him?'

'No — you mean here's there?'

Chris bunched his fist as he heard the news. It was almost unbelievable. 'Mac — didn't you guys keep a look-out like we said?'

'Of course!' came the reply, sounding a little offended, 'I'm telling you Chris, Mick didn't come this way. Just Russell.'

'Damn ...' sighed Chris. 'I was sure this was going to work ...'

'Should we call the police anyway?' Mac asked. He was also carrying his father's mobile phone. Chris really had believed they'd thought of everything.

'What's the point? I was hoping we'd catch him at the house! Now we have no way of telling if he's still there, and according to you we don't even know how he gets in or out.'

Chris had been so sure that Mick would reach the house along the embankment when he saw the smoke. Given the way he liked to keep out of sight, he just couldn't imagine Russell's brother walking along the Graves Road, and any other way was just too long.

They'd blown it. Chris couldn't contain his anger.

'Mac – are you *sure* you didn't see him? What about now?'

Mac didn't sound much more laid-back when he replied. 'I'm telling you, Chris. Mick didn't leave the camp. We saw Russell on the embankment, but that's all. Really!'

'And no-one left the traveller's camp?'

'Only that Greg guy. He left the camp and went tearing up the lane.'

Greg? How did that work? Chris tried to sort the information through in his head, but it just wouldn't come. Finally, he told Mac to head back for the main road and that they'd meet him and Jazz at the bridge.

'This doesn't make sense ...' Chris muttered.

'Is that it?' asked Nicky. 'Shouldn't we just call the cops anyway?'

'No,' said Chris quietly, 'there'll be no-one here by the time they arrive. We've blown it, OK. Let's get out of here before anything else goes wrong.'

He led the way along the edge of the field, following in reverse the route he and Nicky had taken on their bikes at the weekend. As they ran, his mind was racing even faster than his feet, trying to work out why his plan hadn't actually allowed them to catch Mick Jones at the house, and get him out of Russell's life once and for all.

Eighteen

'Because it was a stupid plan, that's why!'

Coming from Fuller that was a bit rich. All the same, Chris said nothing and waited for the big defender/midfield ball-winner to tell them where they had gone wrong.

Most of the crowd in the playground on the Thursday had taken part in the discussion earlier that week. At the centre of the group, Chris, Nicky, Jazz and Mac were sitting on one of the benches outside the upper school toilets, looking very sheepish. They were surrounded by about thirty other kids from middle and upper school. Chris wondered how a plan he and Nicky had first cooked up less than 24 hours ago had become public knowledge. He started to wonder if their English homework that night would be a 500-word essay on Why Chris Screwed Up.

Griff, for example, put it down to the equipment. As far as he was concerned, they had needed much more powerful radios. When he couldn't get Chris to bite on that, he started talking about night sights and infrared cameras. It took a while to remind him that even Mac didn't do that well at Christmas.

Phil Lucas thought the problem was that the plan was so rushed. Once Mac and Jazz had invited themselves on to the team, and Mac had mentioned he had the radios and could probably get his father's phone, it had seemed a good idea to have them as back up. Certainly it had seemed safer than the original plan, in which Chris and Nicky would have been hiding at the house alone, ready to follow Mick when he appeared and to call the police the first chance they got. The only trouble was that the delay while Mac had run home to get the gear meant it was almost dark when Chris and Nicky had lit the fire in the old oil barrel. That only started Griff up about the night sights again.

Some in the group argued Chris and Nicky should have gone it alone; others said there had been no choice but to get Jazz and Mac to watch the camp. In the end, the majority vote came down on the plan being completely useless anyway, which saved a lot of arguing even if it did make Chris feel about a centimetre high.

'Hey,' whispered Nicky, 'we gave it our best shot. We couldn't wait – the game is this Sunday! And we've got practice tomorrow, Friday and Saturday, plus there's the Equinox Fair on Saturday, so . . .'

'It's OK, Nicky, I remember what we decided,' muttered Chris. Now that the group had decided he was an idiot, they were drifting away. Chris nudged Nicky and they made their way over to the snack shop. Chris bought a KitKat, even though there was one in his lunch-box. Nicky, who had eaten his mother's customary four-course lunch, bought a Virgin Cola and a Lion bar and was debating what else to have when Chris pulled him away.

'Have you managed to figure out any more about what happened last night?' asked Chris.

Nicky had a mouthful of chocolate already and couldn't reply, so he rocked his head from side to side in a 'maybe, maybe not' kind of way as he chewed. Chris waited impatiently for his mate to finish.

'I think Mac was at fault on all three goals,' Nicky said. 'The first one definitely; he should have come for the ball befo–'

'Not the football!' Chris cried in anguish. Was Nicky just mucking around or was he really that thick? 'I'm talking about what happened at Russell's house.'

'So am I,' said Nicky, looking hurt and offended. Chris flapped his mouth for a moment, then decided he had to hear what Nicky's logic would be.

'OK, accept the fact Mac didn't do that well last night,' said Nicky. Chris could just about go along with that, but he didn't blame his Scottish friend in any way. After all, Mac had been the team's goalkeeper a while back, and had hated it even though he was a fair shot-stopper. His lack of size made it very hard for him to deal with crosses and anything aimed under the crossbar.

'So, he probably had one of his sulks on. You know what he's like.' Yeah, thought Chris, he's like you. Nicky was still developing his theory, looking up at the sky as he took smaller bites from the Lion. 'So, maybe he had the hump when he should have been watching.'

'But he saw Greg leave the camp,' Chris pointed out, even though the whole discussion was pointless.

'True,' Nicky agreed, stabbing the air with the last stump of the bar. 'So that has to mean he deliberately ignored Russell's brother because –'

Chris really wasn't ready to listen to one of Nicky's conspiracy theories, so he cut his team mate off before he went too far. 'Let's just see what *facts* we can piece together first,' he said with a lot of emphasis on the word 'facts'.

Nicky agreed, and they went across to their school bags to collect some paper. Nicky couldn't think without an A4 pad and a pen at hand. Chris gave him a moment to find a fresh page. He then had to give him another minute while Nicky drew a diagram of Russell's house, showing the yard, the lane and the embankment. He put a neat 'C' in the centre of the house and a small 'N' in the middle of the square that showed the out-house. In the centre of the yard he drew an oil drum belching smoke.

'OK,' sighed Chris at last. 'The first part of the plan worked fine. Russell saw the smoke and came to check out the house.' He drew out a route on Nicky's map with his finger. 'Mac and Jazz saw him on the embankment, coming this way. So, he must have dropped down here, come round through the yard and slipped in through the back door.'

The route passed right in front of the out-house door.

'Are you sure you didn't see him?' Chris demanded.

'No – I told you, I didn't see anyone.'

'Then it must have been Russell who locked you in. He spotted you were there and slipped the bolt across and then –'

'How could he have known I was there?' Nicky demanded. His face showed that he was wondering if Chris was suggesting he'd shown himself.

That same thought had occurred to Chris, but he didn't want to get into it now. 'You're right. Russell couldn't have known we were hiding at the house.'

'So, who was it who locked the door?' Nicky demanded, tapping the pen down on the out-house.

'I don't know, but I heard Russell talking to someone outside the back door, at the same time as all that other noise at the end of the yard.'

'I heard all the banging and stuff,' Nicky insisted. 'It sounded like someone was tearing up the place looking for stuff.'

'Yeah, but what?' asked Chris. They fell silent for a moment, thinking. They got as far as Nicky writing 'What was he looking for?' on the pad, with an arrow pointing to the end of the yard under the embankment.

'OK,' Chris said sharply, realising how quickly time was slipping away, 'try this next bit. Whoever it was locked you in the out-house was already there. He'd have to have been, to see where we were hiding. That's why we never saw him arrive.'

Nicky snapped his fingers. 'Mick!'

'Yeah,' smiled Chris. 'Whatever he was looking for before, when he tore up the house and frightened Marie out of her wits, he didn't find it. So he was there again when we arrived.'

'Yeah!' Nicky said, with even greater enthusiasm, 'and when he saw us arrive, he must have wondered what we were up to. So he locked me in the out-house and came looking for you.'

Chris allowed his mind to race through those moments again. Was that how it happened? He remembered the figure at the door, hammering at it, trying to get in. At the time, he had been sure it was Mick.

'But why . . .?' he said, thinking out loud.

Nicky was writing furiously, adding numbered notes under the diagram. When he'd finished, he looked up, tapping the last one of the points he'd made. 'Because he'd got what he came for — Russell! Think about it. We thought him and Russell had teamed up, but maybe he came back to Oldcester to get him! You know, revenge or something.'

The idea appeared in the front of Chris's brain like a swirling, confusing pattern, or a jigsaw with hundreds of pieces filled in but still no picture. He knew what Nicky was groping towards, but . . .

'That's not it . . .' he whispered.

'OK, not revenge. Maybe he just wanted to get his hooks into Russell again. Maybe he figured his brother would be a success one day; you know? Maybe Russ has already done stuff that Mick never could and he's jealous. Or maybe . . .'

Chris was shaking his head. 'All Russell's done so far is get himself into the youth team scheme. He's still a long way away from fifteen million pound transfer deals or Premiership wages, Nicky . . .'

'Yeah, but the England thing –'

'No-one knows about that except Sean, us and the England schoolboy people. Remember? Russell didn't even know himself until yesterday! He was surprised when I told him.'

'So what then?' cried Nicky. Chris tried to think, tried to see through the wall, but the more he tried the harder it became. Finally he shook his head.

'We're doing it again, Nicky. Every time we try and figure out why, we just tie ourselves up in knots. Concentrate on what actually happened, yeah? Where had we got to?'

'Mick locking me in the out-house,' Nicky read.

Assuming it was Mick, Chris thought, but he didn't say that out loud. Nicky became discouraged so easily if he had to rub any of his points out. Besides, who else could it have been?

'OK,' Chris continued. 'Mick locks you in the out-house. Then Russell slips into the house and . . .' He dried up, unable to say the words.

'. . . then he hid in the closet. What? You know it was him, Chris . . .'

That wasn't the problem. Chris thought it through again, trying to work out the timing of events. 'But if Mick was there first, why didn't he come for me after he trapped you out of the way? Why did he go all around the house to the front door? And how did Russell get into the house, into the closet without Mick seeing him?'

The more he thought about it, the more the questions piled up. Mick would have known about the junk in the hall blocking the door, since he had been the one to throw it all there. And he would definitely have known the back door trick and come in through there if he was in a hurry. It was even closer to the out-house. If the plan was to get Nicky and Chris out of the game and leave a clear run on Russell, why go all the way round the house?

'This is nuts!' Chris said. The whole thing was getting to him.

What other facts could they rely on? That Russell had someone with him? Sure, and that had to be Greg, right? The whispered conversation through the back door, that had been about Greg warning Russell where Mick was, so that they could make their escape. And Greg had unlocked the out-house door to let Nicky run away too. That was it, right?

Almost yelling in rage, Chris gripped a hank of his blond mop of hair in his fist and tugged hard. No, no, no. It still didn't work. Again, how did Greg know where Nicky was? He wasn't there until late on, he wouldn't have seen Nicky slip into his hiding place.

'I just don't get this,' Chris growled. 'It doesn't fit.'

Nicky looked down at the pad, and then back up at Chris. They had never been so frustrated by anything. Nicky looked at his watch – lunch was almost over. Time was running out; time today, time that week. They had less than four days if Russell was going to appear in goal against England.

Chris reached out and took the pad from Nicky. He read the page again, then tore it from the pad and screwed it into a tight ball. His teeth were grinding together.

'We can't get answers like this, Nicky. We have to go back out there again. We've got to talk to Greg and find out what he saw.'

Nicky shrugged as if he agreed, but they both knew there was a practical problem with that idea.

'But when Chris? We've got practice with United tonight and tomorrow, plus more practice and the fair on Saturday, and then –'

'Yeah, yeah,' sighed Chris, 'I know. We're running out of time.' It was going to take something pretty desperate to turn things around. Chris bit his lip hard; Nicky knew at once that his partner had reached a decision.

'Well?'

'Looks like Russell isn't the only one missing practice tonight . . .'

Nineteen

Nicky grumbled all the way. It rained as they went home to get their bikes. He had to tell his mum all kinds of stories about how he was riding to London Road for the training session, and he knew he'd be found out. Plus, for all that he hated working hard, Nicky enjoyed the United coaching sessions.

'Why couldn't we bunk off school?' he moaned.

'We don't have another day to waste,' Chris insisted. 'Besides, if "Andy" Cole caught us bunking off, we'd be banned from training for a month.'

Nicky continued to gripe, even though privately he was admitting to himself that Chris was right. They cycled along the main road and on to the lane, splashing through puddles. Already the evening was darkening, nightfall hastened by clouds as it had 24 hours before. Chris was glad they weren't planning another trip to Russell's house.

'Something else bugging you?' he asked. They were nearing the stile that led across the fields in the direction of the cottage. They both rose out of their saddles and pushed on a little quicker in the direction of the meadow.

'Why?' snapped Nicky. Chris decided to change the subject.

'What's the latest on Marie?' He knew that Nicky had been to visit Russell's sister on a couple of occasions since they had found her. She'd been kept in a couple of nights while the hospital checked her out for concussion and social services tried to find her somewhere to stay. Chris wondered what had happened to her since.

One look over his shoulder at Nicky's face made him wonder if he'd changed the subject after all.

'She's at my place,' Nicky grumbled.

Chris raised his eyebrows. This was news. 'Really? How did that happen?'

'Aw . . .' Nicky moaned, but then he let it all spill out. 'You know what my mum's like. She came with me to the hospital on Monday. She'd bought all kinds of stuff girls need – you know.' Chris had no more idea than Nicky, but they could let that pass. 'I only went because Marie made me promise when I left her on Sunday. So then my mum gets involved and the next thing I know she's told social services Marie can stay with us until her family is found. And Marie says that's what she wants too. So, there you are. Just what I needed, another silly girl at our place.'

Chris thought privately that Nicky had got off lightly. If Mrs Fiorentini had been taking food parcels into hospital, a few dozen patients might have asked to come and stay as well, reckoning they were on to a good thing.

There was already a female cousin and a girlfriend of one of Nicky's cousins staying at the house, along with Nicky's sisters (plus one baby brother), his mum, his gran and whatever other house guests arrived on any one evening. Nicky's dad went out a lot. Nicky tried to do the same.

'They're on about swapping bedrooms again,' Nicky muttered.

Chris knew that this threat had been hanging over Nicky's head for quite a while. Even so, he had fought it off this long. It seemed odd that he was so grumpy about it tonight.

'What?' Nicky cried, seeing Chris looking at him.

'She fancies you!' Chris laughed, inspiration striking at last.

'No! Of course not!' Nicky answered, just a little too quickly to be convincing. He pushed angrily at a twist of hair that fell across his eyes, trying to stuff it under his helmet. 'She's just relying on me because of what happened, you know? I mean, all her family have run off, except for Russell and his psycho brother . . . she needed someone to lend a hand, and my mum's too soft to say no.'

Chris was smirking so widely it hurt his lips.

'I always knew you'd be the first,' he quipped.

Nicky barked something unpleasant and kicked down hard on the pedals, passing Chris at some speed. It took until after they had followed the short stretch of School Lane to catch up with him again. By then, Nicky was back in control, his eyes glistening with anticipation at getting some answers at last.

125

'There's Rat,' he said as they reached the gate. 'Let's hope things start making sense soon.'

Chris hid his grin as best he could. He was keen to get on with asking the right questions. It looked like he had recovered his form in mystery-solving at just the right time.

The only problem with that was that Greg wasn't around to be asked anything.

The small group of travellers seemed to be working quite energetically. Some of them were up at the far end of the meadow, wielding what looked and sounded like a chainsaw. In the camp itself, some of the women were sitting on a long, makeshift bench, baking cakes and biscuits in industrial quantities, which would have been more impressive were it not for the fact that Chris had seen Nicky's mum in action.

When he caught sight of the two boys opening the gate, Rat's face didn't open in a welcoming smile or anything like that. Instead he made a fast move with his hands that threw a cloth over what seemed to be a large square of yellow metal with some writing on it. He advanced towards Chris and Nicky at a brisk pace. If he had only played football that quickly the other day, he would have been on the winning side.

'Hey,' he said as he came up to them.

'Hi,' said Chris. 'Is Greg around?'

'No, he isn't,' Rat replied, and if his face had been less than jolly before, it looked decidedly off-colour now.

'Oh . . .' said Chris, slightly at a loss. 'Any idea where he is?'

'No,' replied Rat. He stood directly in front of them with his arms folded. If that was supposed to prevent them coming any further, it failed miserably. Nicky had smelled the food.

Within thirty seconds, Nicky had charmed the woman who had brought them Coke last time out of some of the ginger biscuits she had been piling into plastic tubs. Nicky managed to make it look like he was earning his keep by filling a few containers, but since he stayed in touch with the food, all that really achieved was the loss of still more of their supplies.

'You guys are busy,' said Chris, smiling slightly at Nicky's nerve. He was still face to face with Rat, just inside the gate.

'Yes, we are,' Rat replied, in a way that suggested he hoped Chris's next word would be 'Goodbye'. When Chris just nodded thoughtfully, the large man added: 'I'm surprised to see you here again.'

'Oh?'

'After that trouble the other day with the police and stuff.'

Chris was about to say that he thought the police were more likely to scare Rat and his people away, but he decided that wasn't the smart way to get any cooperation.

'It's a local tradition,' Chris told him. Rat looked puzzled, so Chris explained. 'The week before the Equinox Mystery Fair, all the kids try to find out where it's going to be held.'

Rat looked back over his shoulder. The bright metal structures supporting the bigger rides and the vivid awnings of the sideshows were clearly visible in the distance. There was even a thumping bass rhythm booming out from one of the attractions testing out its equipment.

'It's hardly much of a secret,' he said, turning back.

'You're missing the point,' Chris said. 'No-one's supposed to know where the fair is until the Friday it opens, but everyone does. It's just a game we go through round here. I bet you've seen loads of kids sneaking around up by that hedge up there...' Chris indicated the distant barrier with a nod of his head. Rat didn't need to look at what Chris was indicating; at that same moment the chainsaw started up again.

'Yeah,' he muttered.

'Of course,' said Chris, 'what none of us have ever thought of before is making our own secret entrance. You've set a new record, Rat.'

Chris's face was a mask of innocence. Rat grimaced uncomfortably all the same. After their previous meetings, Rat had quickly learnt that having Chris around only meant trouble.

'The only thing is,' Chris observed, 'you're making the hole in the wrong place. Where you're cutting, there's the last bit of the farm lane and a big ditch on the other side, not the field where the fair is. You want me to go tell your mates that?'

'Uh...' whimpered Rat unhappily. He looked very flustered now, especially when Chris rode past him, standing in the saddle to push himself up the slight rise. Rat was still frozen to the spot when Chris turned sharply towards the old van, against which were stacked the odd sheets of yellow metal, covered by a blanket. Chris pounced before anyone else could move.

'AA signs?' he laughed, once he had pulled the blanket clear.

Rat looked even more miserable than before.

'That's a new scam,' smiled Nicky from the biscuit-packing table. He had found himself a place on the end of the bench.

Chris flicked through the signs. 'Official parking spaces,' he read. He looked up to the far end of the meadow. 'Let me guess . . .'

Rat slumped back against the side of one of the cars the group travelled in. It didn't take long to get the truth out of him, particularly since Chris had most of it figured out already.

'According to the real signs, everyone leaving Oldcester is expected to go all the way round to the far side, along the A-whatever it is', said Chris, mentally drawing the map in his head. 'But you're going to direct them along the lane and on to the common.' And charge them, what, a quid a time? It could be a nice little earner . . .

'The only trouble is, the lane is too narrow for anyone to go back out while people are still coming in,' Rat said, 'so we're making a hole at the far end to let them go out that way.'

'It'll still be slow getting people off the meadow,' Chris pointed out.

'Just as well they'll have cookies and drinks to sell, then, isn't it?' laughed Nicky.

Chris joined in and Rat managed a thin smile. He didn't seem that bothered about trying to keep the plan a secret any more. In fact, he just looked fed up by the whole thing.

'It'll never work!' Chris cried. 'Don't you think the fair organisers or the police will notice when all the cars go missing? And it isn't going to take them long to track you down, is it?'

'Greg said we couldn't get in trouble. If the police arrived, we could just merge into the background with all the other cars here, and slip away. He said it wasn't illegal anyway . . .'

Chris had no idea if that was true or not, but he suspected it had to be. More importantly, he had thought Greg would have spotted how easy it would be for them to get trapped here.

'So, where is Greg now?' Chris asked, more keen than ever to catch up with the travellers' leader. Rat, though, only shrugged, and pointed vaguely off towards the fair. 'He's got some other scam going with his mate.'

Chris narrowed his eyes a little, paying very careful attention. Greg's 'mate' was presumably the same guy who had been on his pillion that first time the guys saw him. And Chris had a pretty shrewd idea who it had to be, even if he couldn't work out what had brought them together. Rat was walking back towards the tables where the food was being prepared.

'This friend, is his name Mick?' asked Chris, pursuing the big man.

'Yeah, s'right,' said Rat, his mouth full.

OK. It maybe made sense that Mick and Greg had hooked up somehow. Maybe they had met up in jail or something. At the cottage, it must have been Greg that Russell was talking to through the door, right? Greg had to be helping Russell break free of whatever crooked plan Mick had worked out this time.

'Is there anyone else involved in this scam?' Chris asked.

Rat scratched his cheek and thought before he answered. 'Just his kid,' he replied.

'His kid?' asked Chris, his voice rising. 'Greg's kid?'

'Nah . . .'

He meant Mick? Chris felt his heart beating faster.

'Mick's?' he demanded. 'Mick's kid? Or do you mean his kid brother?'

Rat looked flustered at Chris's questions. He moved the scratching finger up to the bald spot on the top of his head. 'I don't think so . . .' he began.

Chris didn't wait for the answer. 'Come on, Nicky, we're out of here,' he said briskly. Nicky sighed, beamed his most attractive smile at the woman in charge of the baking, and left the table with his arms piled with biscuits. How he intended to steer his bike was anyone's guess.

'We got it sorted, then?' he asked. Chris refrained from wondering how 'we' had done anything.

'The fair. That's where we get the answers,' he said, calmly.

Nicky made a disappointed face. 'We're stuck then. Look at them security guys watching Rat's mates at the hedge. There's no way we'll get in.'

'So, it'll have to keep until Saturday,' Chris insisted. 'Whatever's going on, we'll find out then.'

Nicky had managed to climb on to the saddle of his bike, and was opening his jacket to stuff his hoard inside so that his hands would be free.

'Cutting things a bit finer than normal, aren't we?' he commented.

Chris took a moment to reply. He was looking at the row of bikes parked at the edge of the camp, noting how they were all more or less crocked. Greg's was at the end of the row — one of the wheels had been removed. Perhaps the tyres hadn't been able to take the strain of all the rough roads they had visited in the last few days.

'Maybe,' he said at last, 'but at least this time I'm not locked in a cupboard.'

Nicky looked a little confused at Chris's remark, but he had worked it out by the time they got back into Spirebrook. Quite a few other things had been worked out by then too.

Twenty

'So, what have you spotted?' asked Chris's father, catching his son up.

Chris was standing in the middle of the path, looking directly ahead. On every side, the lights of the fair burnt brightly, and music blared through the smoky air. The smells of fast food, roasting chestnuts and the sweet perfume of candy floss hung on the air. The Equinox Mystery Fair roared all around them, but it wasn't hard to work out what Chris was fixed on.

'Penalty shoot-outs!' read Nicky. 'Neat! You know, Russell would have loved this . . .' His voice trailed off for a second before the penny dropped. 'Oh,' he added. 'Right!!!'

The smile was so broad it seemed to join his ears together. Chris's father caught sight of it and lowered his eyebrows suspiciously.

'Round about now is where you tell me something I don't really want to hear, isn't it?' Mr Stephens sighed.

'Not really,' said Chris brightly. 'Hey – look who else is here!'

The small group turned as one to see who he had spotted. Three men were ambling across the grass, having seen the same sign Chris had. No-one recognised the man at the back of the group, who was a tall, fit-looking individual in a plain white T-shirt, joggers and crisp white trainers. The other guys, though, were very familiar. As soon as he saw Chris, the nearest of the three widened his eyes briefly, then frowned and scratched his beard.

'Hi, Sean!' chirped Nicky, brightly.

'Why am I not surprised at this . . .?' Priest groaned. He was looking closely at Chris as he said it.

'I can honestly say it's just a coincidence us meeting up –

131

although you did say you might be here!' Chris insisted, trying hard to put on an innocent smile. Priest looked at Chris as if he was guarding himself against a cobra that was reared up ready to strike. It hadn't escaped him that the rest of the lads were wearing equally idiotic smiles.

He turned his head towards the third man in his small group, then back to the boys.

'I suppose you want to be introduced . . .' he said.

No-one actually answered, but it was obvious it had to happen. Priest took the long way round, though, starting by running through the boys and their parents. He left Chris and Nicky until last.

'These two I mentioned to you earlier,' he said to his companions. 'This is Nicky Fiorentini, and this one's Chris Stephens. They have this strange idea that they might still be on the United youth scheme, but after tonight they'll be lucky to get a place with Stalybridge Celtic.'

'Who?' choked Nicky, just a fraction worried Priest might mean it.

'Exactly,' said Sean. He glared at Nicky to try and put a little more wind up him, but by the look of things Nicky was already too stunned to cope with any more. It was time for the second half of the introductions.

Still watching Chris and the others, Priest gestured towards the man in the T-shirt. 'This is Callum McAllister,' he said, 'the team manager for the England Schoolboys Under-15s squad. It's his mob we'll be facing tomorrow.'

'And some of these lads are in your team, you say?' McAllister asked. Chris was immediately struck by how much stronger his accent was than Mac's. He managed to make the word 'are' sound like it was spelt with a 'u' and at least six 'r's.

Priest indicated the culprits. McAllister took a hard look at Chris and Nicky, as if trying to work out what position they played and how best to neutralise them. He chewed his lip. It looked as if he was on the point of saying something to Chris, but changed his mind. Instead, he leant forward and clapped Robbie James on the shoulder, almost knocking him sideways.

'And you're James, eh? Aye, I've heard a lot about you. I hear Sean's told you about us wanting you to turn up at one of our training weekends at Lilleshall?'

Robbie mumbled something in reply. It was quite possible that he hadn't understood the question — certainly Chris was sure it needed subtitles. All the same, the younger boy managed to look suitably modest.

'How come some Scottish bloke picks the English School-boys team?' Nicky whispered.

'What makes you think he's Scottish?' Chris fired back, which shut Nicky up for a moment.

'Maybe we'll have the pleasure of seeing some of the rest of you next year,' McAllister continued. 'From what I hear, Spirebrook Comprehensive has quite a team.'

'You obviously haven't seen where we are in the table this year,' Chris replied with a weak smile. The 'Brook had started the season with three straight losses and a draw — and a wild game against their arch-rivals, Blackmoor, had been abandoned when they were winning 5–3. A few wins since then had moved them into mid-table, but it was still a big come-down from having been champions the year before.

'Uh . . .?' choked Nicky, making furious gestures with his head. This chatting was all very well, but he hadn't forgotten that there was still one person left to be introduced to the group.

'Oh, sure, sorry,' said Priest, grinning, who had been dragging it out on purpose. He turned to the smartly dressed figure at his side . . . 'Everyone, I'm sure you all recognise Glenn Hoddle.'

They had, but it was still pretty amazing to hear him use the words! The England manager, wandering around the Equinox Mystery Fair, just like that! Unbelievable. Sure, he was wearing a kind of disguise, but it didn't seem likely that a baseball cap over his smartly cut hair and a pair of glasses with coloured lenses would stop anyone recognising him. On the other hand, no-one was pestering him for autographs or anything (well, not up to now, anyway), so maybe it was working.

The England manager looked around nervously. 'Why don't you yell it a little louder, Sean,' he said. 'I think there are some people on the top of the Ferris wheel who didn't hear you.'

Priest made an apologetic face and the whole group moved off the main track, letting Hoddle step into the shadow of one of the stalls. Of course, the fact that he was now surrounded by a pack of excited young men and parents started to draw a little more attention anyway.

'What's he doing here?' gasped Mac to Jazz.

133

'Why don't you ask him yourself?' Priest jumped in, his ears tuned in like radar. Mac blushed and clamped his mouth shut so tightly it was likely he'd never get it open again.

'Well, you know how it is,' said Hoddle, with a slight trace of a smile curving the corners of his mouth. 'After a while all these World Cup qualifiers get a little boring. I thought I'd come and see a real game. So, when Sean told me that you guys were taking on the England Schoolboys, I thought that would suit me just fine.'

No-one really believed the joke, of course, but they all nodded in agreement anyway. Glenn Hoddle could have said he had come to paint the pitch at Star Park pink and they would have all volunteered to help.

Chris, whose mind was working just a fraction better than some of the others, managed to remember that Hoddle and Priest had been mates from their playing days. Their careers overlapped a little, before Sean went off to play a few years in Holland. Chris also recalled that the former Spurs and England midfielder had also played at Sean's benefit game a while back, not long after he'd been named as England coach.

Priest put the boys out of their agony by telling them that although Hoddle was in Oldcester to watch Sunday's game, they needn't start worrying about playing in the World Cup just yet. Well, not the 1998 World Cup, anyway.

'As for tonight, I just thought it would be a grin to take in the fair . . .' said Priest. His voice lost shape as he reached the end of the sentence, as if he had just thought of something else. 'In fact, it wasn't my idea . . .'

He looked at Chris and Nicky closely.

'There's something going on, isn't there?' he demanded.

'No, no!' Chris insisted quickly. Which was sort of true, in that he hadn't thought to get Sean involved in any way. And he hadn't known anything about Glenn Hoddle's visit. That was just a bonus.

Strangely, Priest didn't believe him.

'This isn't some plan? Something to do with Russell, maybe?'

'No!'

Priest caught the way the other boys were looking at each other. Nicky dropped his gaze to the ground, as if he was worried his trainers might have been stolen. Mac made a nervous choking, giggling sound.

'Are you sure?' Priest asked.

Chris opened his mouth to deny it one more time, then offered a long sigh between his gritted teeth instead.

'Well,' he said, in a low voice, 'not a real master plan. But now you're here, I think it might work out just fine.'

They listened as Chris outlined what he had found out, what he was guessing lay behind it all, and what his plan was for setting things right. They had moved off a little way, to a small burger stand which seemed delighted to have drawn such a burst of customers. Once the team mates, their parents, the Oldcester youth team manager, the England Schoolboys manager and the England coach had been fed with hot dogs, burgers and soft drinks from the stand, and theories and tactics from the mind of Chris Stephens, everyone knew what they had to do.

Actually, a few of them thought Chris was barmy and that what they ought to do was call for the men in white coats. All the same, everyone was pulled into the scheme.

Glenn Hoddle was standing behind Sean Priest. His intelligent eyes were focused on Chris as he listened to the tale. They went a little glassy at one point, but that was all. A small warning voice in the back of his head was suggesting that this was the kind of wild stuff that even Terry wouldn't have got caught up in, but it was too late to back out now.

'This is the kid you warned me about, isn't it?' he whispered to Sean.

'I'm afraid so.'

'Good player, is he?'

'Yeah. A natural goal-scorer. Very good with both feet; excellent in the air; a strong heart, good eyes and a sharp brain – on the football pitch anyway.'

Hoddle nodded as he listened. 'So, in ten years or so, you'd see him as a full England player, maybe?'

Priest lowered his voice even more. 'Almost certainly.'

The England coach was still nodding. 'I hope I've retired by then . . .' he sighed.

Chris waited on the path, feeling the slightly spongy ground beneath his feet as he paced back and forwards. There was a hint of more rain in the air. Chris hoped it held off for a while longer – it would be a shame for the fair if a downpour were to fall now.

Ahead of him, there was a queue of people at the booth. A pair of young blokes were at the front, laughing and joking. They were both wearing football shirts – Coventry away and Newcastle United.

Chris studied the entrance to the stall. It was set back between two caravans, as if it had been jammed in at the last second – or as if it really didn't belong there at all. It was so far off the main beaten track that many people must have missed it, which made the queue all the more remarkable.

A passage into the stall had been made by the simple trick of staking out two lines of sticks and fixing sheets along them to make a kind of tunnel. Someone was hidden in the shadows, by the corner of one of the caravans. He was sitting on a stool, collecting money from the players – it was also a good spot to keep an eye out for anyone who might want to ask awkward questions.

The sign that had been rigged up over the entrance was nothing more than another sheet with red and blue painted lettering. Chris read it again.

PENALTY SHOOT-OUT COMPETITION!

THINK YOU CAN BEAT OUR CHAMPION GOALIE?

£2.50 FOR FIVE PENALTIES. SCORE ALL FIVE TO WIN A STAR PRIZE!

Chris found himself doing the maths again. £2.50 a time. Say one person through every three minutes. That's twenty people an hour – £50. The fair was open from early morning to late at night. Call it twelve hours. That was £600. And there had been Friday night, and Sunday to come. Say another £600.

Twelve hundred. A nice little scam. Well worth coming home for.

The previous two participants were walking out along the sheet tunnel, a father and son. Chris could hear the boy angling for another go.

'I got four!' the boy said. 'I'm sure I'd get him next time.'

'Maybe we'll come back later,' said his father. 'Let's take a look over this way first, OK?'

Chris watched them go. Meanwhile, Coventry and Newcastle had disappeared between the caravans, laughing and joking. Seconds later, Chris heard a loud cheer.

Yeah, Chris thought, the trick was to let everyone get three or four. That way they might have another crack at it. It really was a sweet deal. He wondered why Nicky had never thought of it.

Three minutes later, Coventry and Newcastle appeared in the tunnel, on their way out. They weren't laughing any more. Coventry seemed to think they'd been ripped off. Now there's a surprise, thought Chris, stepping forward.

Without hesitation, he went to the front of the queue. No-one protested. The only one to look surprised at his sudden arrival was Greg and he didn't really twig what was going on until he looked up to take Chris's money.

'What's this?' the tall man gasped, peering over the top of his shades.

'Two pounds fifty,' said Chris, crisply, handing over the cash. He turned away to walk down the tunnel. Behind him, he could hear Greg shifting on his seat. Chris knew he wouldn't want to say anything in front of the queue of people. That gave him time to get inside and take a proper look around.

There was a bit more room behind the caravans, of course. The narrow passage widened out into a modest-sized area, ringed off by more sheets. At the far end, there was a ragged net strung up between two trees, presumably to catch wild shots. Below it, there was a five-a-side goal.

That was a small surprise, although Chris realised he should have expected it. The smaller goal stacked the odds even more in favour of the show.

The next thing he saw was no surprise at all. Not for Chris, anyway. Mick, on the other hand, looked completely poleaxed.

'Stephens!'

'Hello, Mick!' said Chris, jauntily.

Russell's elder brother hadn't changed much in the last year or so. He was bigger, perhaps – Chris wondered if he had been using weights in the prison gym. He still wore the same amount of stubble on his chin and his hair was still close-cropped. His dress sense seemed to have taken a dive, though. Chris remembered the smart leather jacket Mick had owned before (it had probably been ruined when he fell in the river); now he was wearing a long brown coat over baggy black trousers and a khaki shirt. It all looked a bit army surplus.

Chris stared at the coat for a moment longer. It was the same sort of thing Russell had worn in the past, back in his thieving days. It had pockets all over the place. Chris suddenly realised Russell hadn't been wearing a coat at all when he saw him at the cottage. It also occurred to him that Russell was very tall for his age, while Mick wasn't a huge amount bigger.

Chris felt cogs turning in his mind. Mistaken identity, he told himself. When he thought he'd seen Russell, perhaps he'd seen Mick. Maybe the same mistake had been made by others too.

Mick was looking at him over the top of the mirror-lens shades he had been wearing when he had passed by Chris on the back of Greg's bike. If only they had recognised him back then, thought Chris. Perhaps Russell had.

'I'm surprised to see you here, Stephens,' Mick said, his voice slightly hoarse and gravelly, as if he had a cold. 'Didn't you get my message?'

Chris was almost up to speed on the mistaken identity thing now. It wasn't Russell who had called at his house and spoken to Dr Loenikov – it was Mick. Warning him off.

'Perhaps it's just a coincidence I'm here,' Chris said brightly. 'I mean, you're running a penalty shoot-out game. You might have guessed some of us might see it and fancy our chances.'

Looking around, he could see someone moving in the darkness behind the goal. The shadowy figure was collecting a ball that had flown wide when Coventry or Newcastle had taken their turn at being fleeced for £2.50. Chris felt his pulse quicken slightly.

'Even so . . .' said Mick after a while, 'it takes a lot of guts for you to be here with me . . .'

He could have added 'after last time', but he didn't need to. If he was trying to freak Chris out by reminding him of all the fun they'd had the last time they were together, he was succeeding. Not by much, but Chris felt as if the temperature had fallen just a little.

'I don't think I'm in any real danger,' said Chris. 'You can't freak me out just because you're a bigger scrum half than me.'

Mick didn't reply (perhaps because he had no idea what Chris was blathering on about). His cagey eyes flickered to the side. Chris didn't react. He had already heard the footsteps approaching from behind.

'What's going on here, Jonesy?' Greg asked, seeing the other two chatting across the width of the small enclosure. Chris finally allowed himself to glance to the side. Greg didn't look very happy. In fact, he looked a lot more uncomfortable than Mick or Chris.

'We're kinda catching up on some old times,' said Mick, his soft, gentle accent managing to hide the menace in his voice. Chris fought the temptation to take a step back.

'You know each other?' asked Greg, although it sounded as if he had suspected as much all along.

'I'm a friend of Russell's,' said Chris, firmly. Mick just smiled.

Greg was nodding his head, as if he was putting a few things together. After all, he'd met Russell when they'd played the game on Horton's Meadow the weekend before. Chris wondered why he hadn't made the connection before.

'So . . . what are you doing here, Chris?' Greg asked.

Chris gave Mick the answer, even though he hadn't been the one asking the question. It seemed really important to let Mick know that he wasn't frightened of him any more, and that he knew what was going on.

'I've paid my two pounds fifty, so I thought I'd try and win a prize. What is it, by the way? Some knocked off sports gear? Stolen football souvenirs? A car?'

Mick was smiling wider than before. Greg coughed. The person behind the goal was coming closer, emerging from the night's dark gloom into the glare of the lights rigged up around the enclosure.

'Hey, Russell. Think you can stop me getting five past you?'

The keeper stepped into the enclosure. Chris's smile faded very quickly. Perhaps this wasn't going to be easy after all.

The goalkeeper was Kim.

Twenty-one

—— ⚽ ——

'I . . . don't get it . . .' Chris gasped.

Mick was still silent. Greg looked more hesitant than ever.

'You thought your friend would be in goal?' asked Greg. 'How come?'

That was a question Chris wasn't prepared to answer for two reasons: first, it would take too long and second, it looked like he was wrong. Chris hated to be wrong. He could feel his stomach churning.

'Score five penalties to win a prize . . .' Mick smiled. He indicated some stuff on a table behind him. Radios, cassette players, football shirts, boots . . . a collection of assorted bits and pieces that might have come from someone's attic but for the fact that it was all in the original boxes.

He kicked the nearest football over towards Chris who trapped it without thinking. Mick nodded towards a small white mark painted on the grass. Kim was watching them all with his normal look of hostility.

'I'm pretty fixed up with football stuff and electrical gear,' Chris said. 'How about you just tell me what's going on?'

Mick shrugged, glancing at Greg. The biker seemed to be shrinking back into the shadows again.

'Shall I tell him, Greg-sy?' Mick asked, still beaming smugly.

'Do you think that's wise?' his partner snapped back, sounding extremely nervous. He was almost back in the entrance tunnel once again.

'Why not?' said Mick, looking increasingly confident and in command. He shifted a little on the seat he was using, turning sideways to flick through the boxes on the table. 'What harm can it do?'

Just in case he was 'it', Chris decided this would be a good time to establish some ground rules. 'I'm not on my own,' he

140

said, watching Mick's reactions carefully. 'My dad and my friends are outside, keeping an eye out.' Not to mention the England coach and United's youth team manager. Chris decided that revealing their involvement might make the threat seem less realistic.

To Chris's disappointment, Mick didn't react badly to the news at all. In fact, if anything, it was Greg who seemed to jump, as far as Chris could tell from the corner of his eye.

'There's no-one outside ...' Greg said, edgily. 'Just a small queue of people waiting to get in.'

'My friends are the queue,' said Chris (and he hoped it was true). He still had his eyes fixed on Mick. 'Why don't you tell me what you've done with Russell?'

For the first time in several minutes, Chris noticed a change in Mick's appearance. A few muscles around his mouth and eyes tightened. He didn't look quite so cocky.

'I haven't done anything with Russell,' he said softly.

'I don't believe you,' Chris returned.

There was a brief silence. The two old enemies faced each other like duellists, seconds before they raised their pistols.

'Take a penalty, Chris. Kim's no Russell, but it ought to be a challenge for you.'

Chris gripped his fists tightly. This was more like Mick; playing games. It would suit him to make Chris play for high stakes. Fine. Just because Kim could play a few tricks with a ball, that hardly qualified him to stop a Chris Stephens bullet.

Chris rolled the ball on to the white spot, lining up on the goal. Mick gestured with his eyes and Kim went between the posts to take guard. He looked very small there.

Chris took a three pace run up, shaped left and hit the ball right. Kim barely moved as the ball flashed inside the post. Without a moment's hesitation, Mick rolled out a second ball.

'Nice effort. Four more to go.'

'Where's Russell?' Chris demanded.

'Greg thought he needed a rest.'

'That doesn't answer the question.'

Mick didn't correct the mistake. Instead he nodded at the ball at Chris's feet.

Fine. Chris lined up again. He didn't doubt that Kim would make a better effort at some of the later strikes, but it had been interesting to note that the boy didn't seem to have bitten on Chris's body language before the first penalty. So, it was probably going to be easier if he concentrated on hitting the ball as crisply and accurately as he could.

He put the second penalty low and to Kim's left, the same side as the first. The boy threw out a foot but the ball went past too quickly.

'You've got better since I saw you last,' Mick observed. He tapped a third ball forward with the toe of his boot.

'I wish I could say the same. Why did you come back, Mick?'

Mick's smile wavered for just a second. His gaze was as hard as crystal, but it was no longer centred on Chris. In fact, he seemed to be looking a long way away.

'This is my home, Stephens. It's where I belong. And one thing I always promised my family was that I would always be here for them, looking out for them. They need me.'

'Yeah, right!' scoffed Chris. 'That's why they've all run away to who knows where. Except Marie, of course. She didn't run away fast enough, and you just knocked her to the ground. She's fine, by the way. And you want to hear something funny? She thought it was Russell who tipped her down the stairs. Because of the coat thing.'

Chris pointed at the faded leather coat Mick was wearing. It was obvious to him now that it was very different from the ratty old thing Russell used to wear, but Chris could imagine Marie, in the dark, frightened out of her wits, not being able to see that.

'You think it was me..?' Mick hissed. Chris nodded. It seemed to take Mick a long while to be able to speak again.

'Take another penalty, Stephens. You're running out of time.'

Chris hit the third penalty to Kim's left again, despite the fact that the tiny keeper threw a dummy to suggest he was going that way. The ball lifted a bit, but Kim was already going the wrong way as the ball whistled into the goal.

Three from three.

'This is all about Russell, though, right?' Chris said. He had to speak loudly, because a burst of music had started from somewhere close by. 'You heard he was doing well at United, so you just had to come back and spoil things. Or were you hoping you could get your claws back into him, so that when

142

he made it big, you'd still be pulling the strings.'

Chris had been warned about mixed metaphors in English class. It was really difficult to avoid using them when he was this het up. He didn't think Mick would correct him.

'Think about it, Stephens. Suppose you had influence over a player, a way of controlling him. Suppose that player went on to be a Premiership goalkeeper, maybe even England's keeper. Think what that might be worth?'

Mick could see Chris was only just beginning to open his mind up to the possibilities. 'What's the matter? Did you really think this sideshow was what it was all about? A weekend scam?' he laughed bitterly. 'Think of all the sponsorship money, the advertising, the marketing . . . You've seen the kinds of deals agents make for players. And that's just the legal stuff. Supposing you had a goalkeeper completely under your control. Suppose you could guarantee that he'd miss a crucial save . . . in a penalty shoot-out, for example.'

Chris knew the stories. There had been an FA investigation into a number of players who might have been involved in illegal gambling deals. There were still rumours that particular games had been thrown; that goalkeepers who seemed to be having an off-day were maybe dropping the ball on purpose.

Nothing could have made Chris feel angrier. In his book, you played for a team because you wanted to help them win. The idea that you'd deliberately lose for a few quid . . . It was like going into the stand and slapping every one of the fans in the face, one by one.

'You'd never get Russell to do that,' he growled.

'You sure about that?'

Chris felt his whole body tighten. He knew he had been thrown off-balance by Russell's behaviour, that he had had doubts. But he knew Russell well enough to be sure that when Russell pulled on his keeper's jersey, he did so because he wanted to be the best. No-one could sink their claws in deeply enough to pull his strings – or anything else, for that matter.

Mick could see what Chris was thinking. 'Russell's not so different from me,' he said, smirking. 'He puts his family first.'

That was true, Chris realised. But did that mean Russell could have been seduced into turning crooked again?

'He walked away from you before,' Chris said firmly. 'He did it because he put his family first. They don't need you any more. And nothing you could have done or said would have changed that.'

He expected Mick to react badly, but in fact Mick seemed relieved and pleased that Chris had reached this conclusion.

'You're starting to get the picture at last, Stephens. I knew you were bright. In fact, I was relying on it.' The smile faded rapidly. Chris knew Mick well enough to treat that as a warning sign. 'Penalty number four.'

Chris trapped the ball Mick kicked over to him. He flicked a glance at the goal, where Kim was setting himself to be ready for the next attempt.

'Think about it,' Mick called. 'We haven't had to give away too many radios while Kim has been in goal either.'

Chris halted, having just placed the ball. What did *that* mean?

Mick was sitting back, arms folded. His smile was broader than ever. 'Go ahead,' he said.

Chris looked at the goal, and the tiny keeper at the centre. He remembered how well Kim moved with the ball. The kid was some athlete. Maybe a reasonable goalkeeper too.

He closed his eyes and banished any such thoughts. Chris knew the rules about penalties. Not just the ones in the FA Handbook about the keeper not moving before the ball was struck, but the *real* rules, the ones that mattered (and were obeyed). Penalties were one-on-one, striker and keeper. They were a game within the game. The advantage was with the striker, who only had to strike the ball accurately and with a bit of power to win 99 per cent of the time.

But that's where the mind games came in. The goalkeeper's job wasn't the diving and the saving – after all, there were only two choices (left or right), and once that was decided, it was just a question of being in the way when the ball arrived. What really mattered was that the keeper could get into the striker's mind. He had to convince the forward *this* penalty was going to be the 1 per cent time.

Do that, and 1 per cent can become 30 per cent, easy.

In a shoot-out, things get even crazier. Keepers can plan a strategy, aiming to stop the fourth penalty, or the fifth, by letting the strikers see what they do with the first three. See? Whichever way I step first, that's the way I'll dive. Then, when the fourth guy steps up, the keeper reverses the movement and — wham! — it's a save.

Chris knew his job was to ignore the keeper. So long as he did his job right, he'd score. He couldn't think about what *might* happen, because then the keeper had won. He just had to step up and STRIKE!!!

Kim got a hand to the fourth penalty. Chris had gone to the other corner, Kim's right, hoping the keeper would expect him to stay with the plan that had netted the first three. In fact, Kim had messed with his head just enough. Chris took a deep breath as he saw the ball cannon off the inside of the post after Kim's fingers had slammed it to the side. That was close.

Penalty head games. If he were Gareth Southgate, would he ever want to take another one again? On the other hand, Stuart Pearce had hit the sweetest of penalties imaginable in both the Euro 96 shoot-outs, despite what had happened in Italia 90. So maybe the best thing Southgate could do was to step up and take every one he was offered.

'That was close,' said Mick. 'Still, four from four. Looks like maybe you win after all.'

Chris was about to say something smart in reply (if only he had been able to think of something), when he heard Greg come back along the tunnel. Chris looked back at him, wondering if there was any way he could get some help from the biker. What he saw made his knees go weak.

'Hey, Chris,' said Russell. 'What's happening?'

'You tell me,' Chris choked.

'OK, look, the game's over,' snapped Greg, edgily. He had his hand on Russell's shoulder. Russell was kitted out in his keeper's kit, even down to the gloves. All Chris could work out in that first moment was that Russell must have been in one of the caravans.

The memory of the cupboard door closing on him made Chris shiver.

'I didn't expect to see you here,' Russell said quietly. Mick laughed.

'Why's that?' Chris asked.

'No, I mean it, we don't have time for this,' Greg growled, sounding more insistent at the second attempt. No-one paid any attention this time either.

'I thought you'd given up on me,' Russell explained in a quiet voice. 'I heard what you said to the police.'

Chris managed to feel guilty for about a billionth of a second. 'I didn't understand what was going on, Russell. In fact, I still don't.'

'Best leave it alone, then, Chris,' Russell sighed. Mick laughed again, even louder.

Greg snapped an angry, worried look in Mick's direction. 'He wasn't kidding about there being others outside. They've even taken down our sign.'

'Game over,' said Chris.

'Not yet,' said Mick, shifting on his seat. 'You've still got one penalty left.' He looked across at his brother. 'You ought to go in goal for this one, Russell. After all, you haven't been beaten five times in a row all day.'

This was getting really weird, Chris thought. He'd always known that Mick was a bit mental, but he was really acting strangely this time. Why bother with the penalty shoot-out now?

'I don't want any of your prizes,' Chris said. 'I know they're all stolen goods; stuff you took before you were arrested.'

Mick let his head rock from side to side, admitting it might be true. 'A few leftovers. They were in the house.'

'Tell me something I don't know,' said Chris. 'That's why you came back, to look for them. I've been to the cottage, Mick. I've seen how you tore your own house to pieces looking for all that junk.'

'It's a mess, all right,' Mick admitted. 'Funny thing, really. You would have thought I'd know where it all was . . .'

'Yeah, ri–' Chris began. And then he felt a cool breath of wind pass over his skin, as if he had been touched by the arm of a passing ghost. A small warning bell was ringing at the back of his mind. It wasn't as loud as the alarm that had been going off at regular intervals since the first moment he saw Mick, but it was trying to get his attention all the same.

Greg was moving towards the back of the stand, where there was just open field and then the hedge at the edge of Horton's Meadow. He was steering Russell ahead of him. Mick moved fractionally, and Greg pulled the younger Jones closer, as if trying to shield him . . . or something.

'We're leaving, Mick,' said Greg. 'The game's over.'

'Don't you want the rest of the money?' asked Mick, rising to his feet.

Greg seemed to have other things on his mind. He pulled Russell closer still, and they took a few quick steps across the grass.

'Keep it,' snapped Greg. 'I've got £250 right here. Not bad for a couple of day's work. That and a car from the common will do me just fine.'

Mick was moving slowly towards them. Greg and Russell were walking quicker across the trampled grass, passing across the goal. As they came closer, Chris saw Kim flinch, looking from Greg to Mick then back again. Then he took a step away, towards Mick.

It was like watching a film of an explosion run backwards. All these pieces were flying together, towards the centre of the blast. But they were still just pieces, unrecognisable junk, right up to the last moment when they became the whole thing once again.

Chris took the last penalty. He'd never hit one truer or harder.

Russell's instincts were as finely tuned as ever. As the ball flew at his head, he caught the flight from the corner of his eye and ducked. Chris could see Greg's hand fixed in the back of Russell's collar. As the keeper pulled down, Greg was dragged forward just a fraction before his strength allowed him to start pulling back.

But by then the ball arrived.

It caught Greg on the corner of his jaw, a solid crack that he never saw coming until the moment it arrived. The impact snapped his head back, pitching him over into the goalmouth. He slid on the wet grass, almost ending up in the net. Russell went down too, but the grip on his shirt had been knocked free. He picked himself up and started to move away.

'Kim, Russell – run!!'

The two of them obeyed Mick's command without question, scooting down the tunnel at breakneck speed. That left just Chris and the two men plus the ball spinning at Mick's feet. With a slow, steady movement, he tapped it into the goal.

'Five from five,' he said, with a momentary glance at Chris. 'We have a winner.'

Twenty-two

Greg's feet were scrabbling on the floor as he fought to get up. The wet ball had left an oval mark along the side of his face. It appeared to have made him a little cranky as well, judging by the look in his eyes.

'What did you do that for?' he shrieked.

Chris didn't explain – he couldn't. Something had been nagging him about Greg for some time. Or perhaps it was that the evidence wouldn't stack up neatly against Mick. In either case, that slight movement Kim had made away from Greg and towards Jones had clinched it somehow.

Mick moved towards him, his hands gripped in tight fists. That made Greg move even faster. He got to his feet and started to run for the hedge.

Mick was on the point of following him, and there was no doubt in Chris's mind that Russell's brother would have caught him easily. In fact, he had no doubts left about anything.

'Leave him, Mick!' he called. As if by magic, Mick stopped immediately. Greg didn't stop to say thank you on his way to hurdling the sheets at the back of the stall and disappearing into the night.

Mick looked back at Chris, still coiled ready for action. He slowly relaxed, then rubbed the back of his neck, stretching his head up as if to release the tension.

'I admire your sense of fair play, Stephens,' he said, with a trace of mockery in his voice, 'but don't you think letting him run off with the money was just a little generous?'

Chris shrugged. He was pretty sure that Greg's escape plan wouldn't turn out as well as the biker might have hoped. After all, his Suzuki was crocked. If he was hoping to steal a car off the common and make his getaway like that, he was in for a big surprise. Even assuming Rat hadn't abandoned the car park scam, the rain over the last few days would have turned the common into a soggy marsh. Any car that had been parked there would need skis instead of wheels. And by now, Priest would be using the mobile phone he always carried to alert the police.

'Well, did I perform the way you expected?' asked Chris. Mick grinned. Well, thought Chris, it wasn't like I thought I'd get an apology.

'Pretty much. You were nosy, obstinate and pig-headed. Pretty much what I'd hoped.'

Chris made a 'Yeah, you too' face. He could hear people running towards them up the tunnel. His father beat Priest and Nicky by a short head. Once he'd let them know he was all right, Chris turned back to face Mick.

'Do I get to hear the whole story now?'

Mick seemed to think this was very amusing.

'You just can't stand the idea of not knowing everything, can you?' he asked. All the same, now that the small area was filling up with other people, including some individuals who weren't among his biggest fans, it was in his best interests to set the record straight. He walked back towards the chair he had been sitting on, and prepared to tell his tale.

'I met Greg while I was on remand. He was in for tax disc evasion. We got talking, and I told him about Russell and how he was doing at United.'

Chris wondered how he knew, but guessed someone in the Jones family had kept in touch with Mick, even after what they had all been through. In fact, it might even have been Russell himself. Chris looked over at his mate, who was near the front of the pack, and saw Russell was wearing the look he always wore when his family's secrets spilled out.

'Then Greg got interested in the Equinox Fair, and we talked about the kinds of scams you could pull. Round about then, he got released. He said he'd come this way with some mates of his to see if they could make some money.

'About a month later, he came to see me again. He told me they'd thought it over, and that although there was some stuff they could do at the fair, they were more interested in what Russell was doing. You see, Greg knows a bit about dodgy football betting. He used to play in Australia, back in the eighties, up until his knee got banged out of shape. He said some guys from Hong Kong offered him money to set up a game that finished exactly four-two. He tried it, but the ball wouldn't run right for the team that was supposed to get four, and the game finished three-three. The Hong Kong guys were very angry and gave Greg a hard time.

'So, I told him all about Russell, and he starts to thinking how having a goalkeeper in on the deal would be the best way to cheat. It's a long term investment, but what the heck, eh? And because of what had happened in the past, he thought I'd be able to get Russo onside.'

'So you thought you'd join in,' sneered Nicky.

Mick was still wearing his relaxed, easy smile.

'Sure, and that's what I did think — for about a second. Then I realised that I'd be making a big mistake. If I let someone else get their hooks into Russell, what kind of man would I be? I've always kept an eye on my family. You may not like me for what I've done, but I've always looked out for them.'

There was a brief pause while Mick looked around to see how many people believed him. It was probably a short list.

'Anyway, that didn't suit Greg. So, while I'm inside, he's after coming this way himself, to see what might be done. And I get to hear about it.

'Now, by this time, the police are having a little trouble making all the charges against me stick. So, I explain to them that I have a family problem I have to attend to, and that I'm prepared to make a deal. I'll confess to some of my misdeeds in exchange for bail up to the trial. And they went for it. Oh, sure, I had to accept a lot of conditions, but it got me out of prison just in time.

'Things get a little complicated after that. I hooked up with Greg and that lot again, said I'd help them with the fair scam. But mostly I wanted to make sure Russell didn't get caught up in anything he couldn't walk away from. But what I hadn't counted on was that Greg was prepared to play dirty.'

'What do you mean?' Chris urged.

'He made it quite clear that he was in charge, and that he was going to take most of the money. And if I didn't play along, he said he'd come back this way after I was sent to prison and harm my family. What could I do? I knew I'd be going away for a few years soon enough. Also, Greg had found another lever to hold against me. Kim.'

Chris was taken aback. 'Kim?' Where did he fit in?

'I had a child with a woman from round here a few years back. Another little secret I told Greg I wish I hadn't. I tell you, when the lights in your cell go out, you have an awful lot of time to talk!

'Kim's mother was short of money, so Greg promised to give her some if the kid travelled with me for a while. Now he had someone else he could use against me. It made life rather . . . difficult.'

Well, that was a twist Chris hadn't expected, although it did make a few other things click in his mind.

'So when did you make contact with Russell?'

Chris could tell at once that Mick liked the answer to this question. 'Well, that's what's so funny. Here am I, trying to stall as much as I can, and then what happens but you, Russo and the rest of your little crew roll up here, large as life — and start playing football! I had to pull a fast disappearing trick off the back of the bike, I can tell you. In fact, that was what made Greg lose his balance and almost run Nicky down. Anyway, later that day, I tipped the wink to Russo when the ball came over by where I was hiding — and it freaked him out.'

That was an understatement, Chris thought.

'That was always my problem. Because of the football thing, Russell couldn't just disappear, so Greg could always find him if he wanted. I had to find a way to drive him off. But after I spoke to him, Russell vanished for days.'

Russell was suddenly at the centre of attention. He had a very sheepish expression on his face, but he didn't offer any answer about where he had been hiding. It wasn't beyond Russell to live rough for a few days.

Mick was continuing his tale. 'I managed to get word to my da to take the family away. They left the cottage just in time, since Greg was on his way to pick up the stuff I'd told him was there. Stuff I'd nicked before. Trouble was, they couldn't find Marie before they went. She came back to the house while Greg was there. He must have scared her, or something, and made her fall. She locked herself in the closet.'

'She thought it was Russell smashing the house up,' said Chris. 'And I thought it was you, because of the coat.'

Mick looked at his chest, remembering what he was

wearing. 'Ah, now this is Greg's anyway. I've been borrowing it while I was on the bike.'

Poor Marie. She must have only caught a glimpse of the coat when she stumbled on Greg wrecking the place. Chris was sure the idea of Russell becoming as berserk as his brother must have freaked her out.

Mick moved the story along. 'Then you pulled that stunt with the fire at the cottage, trying to attract Russell's attention.'

Chris winced. He could feel his father stiffening behind him. There were going to be a few awkward bits to explain when he got home.

'I knew it was a trap, so I intercepted Russell when he arrived. I locked your man Nicky in the outside bog to keep him out of the way, and I was just coming to get you when Greg arrived. I couldn't let him see I was working against him, so I kept out of sight while Russell came after you. Greg didn't manage to get the back door open – how could he, he didn't know the trick – so he went to the front. When that wouldn't open, he started searching the yard for stuff – it was the only place he'd not looked before.'

'So it was you I heard talking to Russell?'

'Not quite. It was Kim.'

Who Nicky hadn't seen because the kid didn't come up to the top of the door. Neat.

'The rest you can work out. I explained things to Russell. He agreed to go along with Greg's penalty scam. Greg's idea was that once Russell had been dragged into one shady deal, it would be easy to blackmail him into more. By the time he turned pro, he'd be ripe for throwing matches and stuff.'

'And your plan was?'

'My plan was to make it look like some nosy kid had stumbled on the whole thing and blown it wide open. I didn't doubt you'd get involved, sooner or later. Particularly if I warned you not to.'

'I think we all could have guessed that,' said Chris's father. Sean Priest uttered a knowing laugh as well.

'I'm guessing Greg will think too many people know what's going on to try anything now,' smiled Mick. 'I think Russo's in the clear.'

There was a lot of conversation buzzing around at this point. There were still questions to be asked, details to be picked over. Certain individuals still thought Mick had been out of order acting the way he had. Chris, on the other hand, was feeling pretty good about it. OK, there was the oil drum/fire business to wriggle out of, plus Sean Priest would be bound to remind him of the conversation they had had in his office, but on the whole Chris felt he'd come out well on top.

'You'll keep an eye on Russo for me, won't you now, Mr Priest?' Mick asked the United coach.

Sean's voice was as cold as ice. 'You can bet on it.'

'And who'll make sure Marie gets back home safely?'

'Nicky will take care of that,' said Chris. 'They've become very . . . close since the accident.'

Mac burst into a fit of the giggles. Nicky glared at him with a murderous look in his eyes. That only started Jazz off as well, and after a while the laughter had spread to Chris, Russell and one or two of the adults.

'And what about Kim? Will someone see her back to her mother?'

'I'll look after that,' said Chris, quickly. 'Just make sure I have the address.' He stopped. Everyone seemed to have gone a little quiet. Chris replayed the last part of the conversation through his mind again. 'Her?'

'Sure, Mr Detective,' laughed Mick, 'hadn't you realised that Kim is my daughter?'

Chris looked round at the smaller of the two goalkeepers. Kim was staring right back at him, with that same manic intensity he – she – always wore. Funny. Now that he knew, Chris could see the resemblance between Kim and her father. A pity he hadn't spotted it before. That and other things.

'Perhaps you and Nicky could double-date?' whispered Mac, who was having much too much fun all of a sudden.

'I'll make sure she gets home, Mick,' snapped Chris quickly. But when he looked, the stool was empty. Everyone realised Mick had gone in the same moment. Chris walked over to the table. He guessed Mick must have a couple of hundred quid in his pocket from the penalty scam . . .

'And since I scored my five out of five . . .' he told himself, reaching out for a pair of Predators.

'So, are we done here?' asked Mac's mum. Everyone agreed it was time to let the police wrap up what was left. Almost everyone, anyway.

'Hold on,' said Sean Priest. 'I'm tired of you kids making a fool of me every two minutes. Well, now this is my moment for a surprise. Russell, this guy is Callum McAllister. He picks the England Schoolboys team. One of the reasons he's here this weekend is to take a look at you and Robbie James. For some reason he thought you might be worth considering for a place at their next training session.'

Russell looked suitably impressed. At the same time, he couldn't help but notice that Sean was speaking in the past tense. He could tell by the way Robbie James was beaming with pride that the training session earlier that Saturday had gone well. Had he missed his chance?

'Am I still . . . playing tomorrow, Sean?' he asked.

Priest shook his head. 'I don't think that would be fair, do you, Russell? The rest of the squad have worked hard this week and Frasier Gillespie has earned his chance. I'm afraid the best I can do is put you on the subs' bench.'

Chris was among the first to say this was unfair, but Russell accepted Priest's view without argument.

'Of course, I'll try to get back for another look at you later in the season,' said McAllister.

'Hang on!' cried Chris. 'Why wait? We're all here now. And we have the equipment.'

The whole group found themselves checking out the goal. Priest looked at McAllister; the England Schoolboys manager shrugged back.

'Fine,' said Priest. 'OK, Russell, you think you're up to keeping out a few penalties?'

Russell slammed his hands together. 'You bet!' He was chuckling as he made his way towards the goal, running backwards. 'I can't see anyone here who's managed to put five penalties in a row past me all season!' he laughed.

Chris had gone to the back, and was leading someone forward. Russell's smile faded very quickly.

'Hey Russell, look who else is here . . .' said Chris, and everyone stood back, their faces lit by broad smiles, as they waited for Russell to show what he could do against the England coach.

'What do I get if I win?' asked Hoddle.

'I know where there's an old motorbike going cheap,' said Chris.

TEAM MATES

WE NEED YOUR HELP . . .

to ensure that we bring you the books you want —

— and no stamp required!

All you have to do is complete the attached questionnaire and return it to us. The information you provide will help us to keep publishing the books you want to read. The completed form will also give us a better picture of who reads the Team Mates books and will help us continue marketing these books successfully.

TEAM MATES QUESTIONNAIRE

*Please **circle** the answer that applies to you and add more information where necessary.*

SECTION ONE: ABOUT YOU

1.1   Are you?

      Male / Female

1.2   How old are you?   .... years

1.3   Which other Team Mates books have you read?

      Overlap
      The Keeper
      Foul!
      Giant Killers
      Sweeper
      Offside

1.4   What do you spend most of your pocket money on?
       (Please give details.)

       Books _____

       _____

       Magazines _____

       _____

       Toys _____

       _____

       Computer games _____

       _____

       Other _____

       _____

1.5   Do you play football?
       Yes / No

1.6   Which football team do you support, if any?

       _____

1.7   Who is your favourite football player, if you have one?

       _____

_____

SECTION TWO: ABOUT THE BOOKS

2.1   Where do you buy your Team Mates book/s from?
                 W H Smith
                 John Menzies
                 Waterstones
                 Dillons
                 Books Etc
                 A supermarket (say which one) _____
                 A newsagent (say which one) _____
                 Other _____

2.2 Which is your favourite Team Mates story and what do you like most about it?

_____
_____
_____

2.3 How did you find out about Team Mates books?

Friends
Magazine
Store display
Gift
Other _____

2.4 Would you like to know more about the Team Mates series of books?

Yes / No

If yes, would you like to receive more information direct from Virgin Publishing?

Yes / No

If yes, please fill in your name and address below:

_____
_____
_____
_____

2.5 What do you find exciting and interesting about the Team Mates stories?

_____
_____
_____

SECTION THREE: ADDITIONAL INFORMATION

3.1   Are there any other comments about Team Mates you
      would like to make?

      _____

      _____

      _____

      _____

_____

*Thank you for completing this questionnaire. Now tear it out of
the book – carefully! – put it in an envelope and send it to:*

**Team Mates
FREEPOST LON 3453
London
W10 5BR**

No stamp is required if you are resident in the UK.